COAY

Tales of Enchantment

By Darién Irizarry

First Edition
ISBN: 979-8-9991017-0-9
Cover & Illustrations by Darién Irizarry
Authored by Darién Irizarry
Edited by Gabrielle Esposito
Published by *DI501 Print* (Subsidiary of *DI501 Industries*)

Timeline of Puerto Rican History

- **c. 1000 AD** – The Indigenous Taíno people inhabit Borikén (present-day Puerto Rico) and adjacent Caribbean islands, developing a complex society based on agriculture, fishing, and hierarchical leadership under *caciques* in settlements known as *yucayeques*.

- **1493** – Although not the first, Christopher Columbus claims Puerto Rico for Spain on his second voyage to the east; the island is named San Juan Bautista.

- **1508** – Spanish colonization begins when Juan Ponce de León establishes Caparra. The implementation of the *encomienda* system led to the decline of the Taíno population.

- **1511** – A short-lived indigenous uprising is suppressed by Spanish forces, marking the collapse of organized resistance.

- **1530s–1700s** – Puerto Rico becomes a strategic military outpost for Spain; African slaves are introduced to replace Taíno labor.

- **1797** – Spanish and Puerto Rican militias successfully defend San Juan from British attack, reinforcing colonial loyalty.

- **1868** – *Grito de Lares*: An unsuccessful but symbolic revolt against Spanish rule; becomes a key moment in the Puerto Rican nationalist movement.

- **1873** – Spain abolishes slavery in Puerto Rico, part of broader liberal reforms in the late 19th century.

- **1898** – Spanish-American War commences when the United States invades Puerto Rico; the Treaty of Paris cedes the island to the U.S., ending four centuries of Spanish rule.

- **1917** – The Jones-Shafroth Act was enacted, which granted Puerto Ricans U.S. citizenship; established a locally elected Senate and extended U.S. laws.

- **1950** – Armed revolts and uprisings in Jayuya and Utuado seek independence; suppressed by U.S. military forces.

- **1952** – Puerto Rico becomes a U.S. Commonwealth (Estado Libre Asociado), with its own constitution and increased self-governance.

- **2012, 2017, 2020** – Non-binding referendums show increasing support for U.S. statehood, though low turnout and political controversy limit impact.

- **2017** – The Category 4 Hurricane Maria devastates the island, causing massive destruction; the federal response was widely criticized, exacerbating economic and infrastructure crises.

- **2021–Present** – Economic recovery efforts, population decline, and debates over political status and self-determination continue to shape Puerto Rico's future.

Legend:

Borikén..1

Coquí...4

Salcedo..8

Yuiza..15

Yunque..21

Sotomayor y Guanina..27

La Piedra Taina...31

Vejigantes...36

Sirena...44

Cofresí..52

El Puente...55

Garita del Diablo...61

Manatí..66

Calle del Cristo...74

Azucar..79

Fantasma...84

Bruja...92

Monstruo...105

Nieve..113

Bomba..117

Grito Boricua..125

Forward

The tales you are about to encounter are rich with love, tragedy, and enchantment. As is tradition, many of these stories were passed down to me through the generations, shared by word of mouth. Over time, these stories have shifted and changed, shaped by collective memories, perceptions, and the world at large.

Puerto Rican history and heritage are often overlooked or erased. This is why many of these stories arrived with gaps and contradictions, which I felt compelled to address. As a child, I would use my imagination to fill in these blanks. Now, as I commit these stories to paper. I have woven together historical truths, classic folklore, and my own creativity to bring these beautiful tapestries of words to life. Though these stories may not align with your own memories or tastes, I hope you find joy in them and take with you the wisdom they offer.

Like all old tales, they are steeped in darkness and messy realities. It is through the trials, misfortunes, and adversities of their characters that we find lessons; lessons that allow us to grow. For those brave enough to delve into what it truly means to be Boricua, I welcome you.

BORIKÉN

From the swirling primordial waters of the cosmos, Atabey gave birth to herself. She, the supreme goddess of creation, embodied everything that was and would be. She created the heavens, separating them from the sky and the earth, and extended them across the boundless universe. In her solitude, she decided to create eternal companions who could bask in the radiance of all she had brought into existence. So, she gave birth to two sons.

These twin boys looked similar, yet they could not have been more different: Yucahu, a god of creation like his mother, and Guacar, a god of weather. Yucahu shaped his mother's vastness with love, creating the earth and filling it with verdant life. He sculpted the mountains and valleys, and with a single breath, commanded the oceans and rivers into being. He populated the land, sea, and even the sky with all sorts of plants and creatures. In his divine power, Yucahu called forth the sun, *guey*, to shine upon all that was good, and *karaya*, the moon, to watch over the night. Boinael and Maroya emerged from a cave and were tasked with their care. The celestial stars, Achinao, Coromo, Racuno, and Sobaco, were made to keep them company.

Yucahu danced through his creation, content, and ensuring that every detail was perfect, imbued with beauty and goodness. Despite his pride in all he had created, there was one creation he considered the greatest of all: the *Locuo*, the first human, a being who mimicked the shape of the gods but was made of flesh and spirit. The *Locuo* was meant to walk, work, and enjoy the lands of Borikén.

From his isolated perch, Guacar, the god of weather, grew envious. Yucahu had the power to create, to command life and light, while he, the god of wind and weather, had limited powers. His heart turned cold, and jealousy twisted into fury. He rejected creation and became its destroyer. Taking the name Juracan, the god of hurricanes, he joined forces with his wife, Guabancex, the goddess of storms and discord, and his adoptive sons, Thunder and Lightning. Together, they brought chaos and destruction to all below the sky.

As the winds of Juracan began to howl, they tore across creation, ravaging crops and sending animals fleeing in fear. The skies darkened as lightning cracked the earth. Juracan's fury left death and ruin in its wake, a constant opposition to all that was good. The humans cried out in despair, but his destruction was relentless.

From then on, Yucahu's creation and Juracan's destruction would remain forever opposed. The struggle between brothers would echo across the land of Borikén, where its people would always rejoice in the blessings of the land, yet fear the great, unpredictable tempest that loomed over them.

Coquí

Coqui was a deeply devout Taino, as was everyone in his *yucayeque*. But among them, he was the most rigorous in his prayers. He would pray not only for the crops, his family, and the hunt, but for something as seemingly insignificant as the sunset. After a long day, he would take the time to offer reverence to the sun as it sank behind the horizon. To Coqui, the value of the setting sun lay not only in its beauty but also in what it symbolized: the promise of a restful sleep and the hope of a new day to come.

Coqui followed this routine throughout his adolescence, and it continued into his adulthood. As he matured, it became evident to everyone that in return for his many years of unwavering piety, the gods had bestowed upon him a pure, virtuous soul and an extraordinarily handsome face. With raven-black hair, amber-colored eyes, and golden skin, there was no doubt that he was the most desired man in the *yucayeque*. Soon, fathers began urging their daughters to compete for the chance to unite with him. Despite their efforts, no one could capture his heart, nor even gain his attention. Coqui was simply too busy, too overwhelmed by his devotion, to consider anything else.

Slowly, the people gave up hope. They believed that Coqui, despite the gods' gifts, was destined to waste away with only a legacy of beautiful thoughts and pious words, inevitably dying alone.

But elsewhere in the heavens, someone had been watching him very closely for a very long time. The goddess of the dawn and dusk, who received his evening prayers with both gratitude and curiosity, had taken notice of his devotion. Coqui's consistency and beauty ignited something deep within her, and soon, the goddess found herself falling in love with him.

One evening, as Coqui made his customary trip to the beach for prayer, he was captivated by the landscape and the waves. Deciding to swim, he waded into the water, unaware that the goddess was watching from above. The twilight reflecting on the water glistened off Coqui's body as if adorned by the stars themselves. The goddess stirred. She could no longer resist the urge to act upon a dangerous thought she had entertained for some time: to introduce herself.

With quiet grace, she shed her godly attire and descended to the beach in the form of a young Taino woman. She joined Coqui in the water, and though he had never seen her before, he felt an undeniable sense of familiarity. She was the most beautiful woman he had ever seen. For someone who had rejected thoughts of love so many times before, Coqui now found himself thinking of only one thing: This beautiful stranger will someday be mine.

The two met frequently at that same beach. Each evening, their souls grew ever more entwined. Eventually, Coqui longed to bring her back to his *bohío* and show her off to his neighbors. But the goddess, torn between her love for him and her celestial duties, struggled with a difficult decision. Part of her wanted to sacrifice her immortality to remain with him, while another part knew the importance of her role in the heavens. After much deliberation, she finally agreed. In her eyes, the world could live without the dawn and the dusk, but it would be rendered meaningless without love.

As they made their way back to the *yucayeque*, a sudden foreboding feeling gripped Coqui. They began to run, but just as they did, the sky unleashed rain and fury. The wind howled, trees were ripped apart, and visibility was nearly impossible amid the storm's destructive force. In the confusion, their hands separated, and the tempest carried them further and further apart. The goddess, in her human form, was helpless against the storm's might.

When the tempest finally subsided, she no longer knew where she was, nor where Coqui had ended up. Desperately, she wandered on foot for days in search of her lost love, calling his name repeatedly with no answer. But when love is as powerful as theirs, one does not simply give up. She made her way back to the beach and remembered who she was.

The goddess realized she would have to look farther and harder than ever before. From the golden sand, she sculpted a tiny frog, then another, and then an entire army. The frogs had large, vigilant eyes, and their colors allowed them to blend into their surroundings. The perfect

7

soldiers and spies for her righteous mission. She breathed life into each of them, imbuing them with a singular command: to spread out across the island and search for her love, calling out his name.

With her plan set in motion, the goddess, now bejeweled with comets and draped in ombré clouds, returned to the sky. From her new vantage point, she could see more clearly, orchestrating the search from above.

Years passed, and Coqui was never found. But the goddess, consumed by her grief, refused to abandon the search. So even to this day, from dusk till dawn, one can hear the distant chorus of her tiny frog soldiers calling his name: "Coqui, Coqui, Coqui."

Salcedo

Captain Salcedo had sailed farther than any man in his fleet. His ship was a proud monument to Spain's naval prowess and its pursuit of expansion, cutting through unknown seas toward an unknown world. The wind whispered promises of riches, untold treasures, and a land seldom touched by civilized hands. He had sailed into the New World, a place as strange as a dream, where the hills emerged from the sea to meet him. Now, on the shores, the land stretched before him in startling silence. Unlike Spain, it was lush and wild, yet sharp in its unfamiliarity. The air was thick and humid with the scent of salt. Towering trees, as thick as the bow of a ship, stood still like silent sentinels, guarding their territory.

Salcedo was not a man to be daunted by such things. He had seen enough on his voyages to the east to know that new lands breed opportunity, gold, spices, and unknown delights that could be traded or turned into profit. His mind raced with the possibilities. He would help make this place the jewel of the Spanish territories.

And so, he made camp along the tree line near the shore, while his men set up their tents and carried the heavy chests of equipment to land. It was then that he saw them, the natives. Not fierce warriors as he had expected, but curious figures who regarded his arrival with cautious yet tempered interest. Their skin was dark, like the fertile earth itself, and their eyes were full of the kind of wisdom one only finds in those who have lived without the chaos of the outside world. They watched from a distance, their bodies draped in simple garments made from hemp and garnished with seashells; clothing that was dull in color but contrasted sharply with their brightly painted faces.

Salcedo had expected hostility and prepared for war, but found instead a peaceful, patient people. There was no hostility, no drawn bows, no war cries, only silence. For a moment, he felt something stir within him, a kind of reverence for these strangers. But then, ambition crept in, dark and insidious.

He knew that they were uneducated in worldly ways and could surely be manipulated. Like naïve children, they would believe anything he told them. So, Salcedo stood tall in his armor, a gleaming silver silhouette in the sun, and spoke words in his tongue, which the natives could only assume to be the language of the heavens. They had never seen a man such as him, so he must not have been a man at all, but a god.

Salcedo could tell from the awe on their faces that he had succeeded in his deception. He let them believe what they wanted and waited to reap the benefits. They brought him gifts of fresh fruit, roots, and impressive carvings. He accepted them with a gracious smile, playing the part he proudly thought he deserved. He ate their food, basked in their offerings, and revelled in their worship.

Days passed, and Salcedo grew comfortable and complacent. He feigned divinity with increasing ease, enjoying the lavish treatment. The natives seemed content to serve him, their belief in his godhood unshaken. Yet beneath this veneer of luxury, a small seed of doubt began to grow in the heart of the chief of a village not far from where the conquistador resided.

Urayoán was a man of wisdom, a leader who had seen many seasons pass, and he was not so easily fooled. He had observed the Spaniards closely, and something wasn't quite right. A culture based mostly on community and trade now witnessed these "new gods" take gladly but offer nothing in return. These visitors ate, slept, and cut down trees without regard. This selfish behavior did not align with the natives' understanding of the divine.

Not many others shared his concerns, which meant he would need to find proof. Urayoán devised a plan, one that would conclusively determine if these strangers were who they claimed to be. He invited Salcedo to visit his village, a humble invitation masked by a gesture of friendship. He spoke of a sacred site, a river deep in the jungle, where the gods were said to have once bathed. Salcedo, eager to maintain the illusion of godhood, accepted without hesitation. He imagined himself standing before the sacred waters, the natives once more bowing before him in reverence.

The journey was long and arduous. Salcedo had never ventured this deep into the island before and found himself to be out of his element. The hot and humid conditions of the jungle made him break out in heavy sweat. As they journeyed, he constantly tripped over the twisted roots of the trees. The jungle was alive with the sounds of birds calling out in strange echoes and the

11

rustling of unseen creatures in the underbrush. In Salcedo's exhausted misery, he began to question if he had made the right choice.

When they reached the river, its waters shimmered with a strange, unnatural beauty. It was a quiet place. The only sound was the gentle flow of water over stones. Salcedo looked out over the river and saw natives standing at a distance, their expressions unreadable. Urayoán approached him and gestured toward the river as if suggesting a ceremonial refreshment. Salcedo, thirsty and dirty, eagerly stumbled into the water, feeling instantly refreshed. After a soak and a drink, he lay back in his armor, floating above the water and watching the canopy sway in the wind.

Without warning, the natives closed in, their hands strong and swift. Before Salcedo could react, they submerged him in the sacred waters. Panic surged within him as he realized that he had indeed made a mistake. Had they seen through his facade? Was he to be remembered as a failure? Was this the end? His mind raced, but there was no escape. The water that had quenched his thirst was now cold, aggressive, and forcing its way into his lungs.

The world blurred, and then darkness.

For days, Salcedo's body lay still in the river, his lifeless form carried by the currents while the Taíno people watched attentively in silence. Some hoped that he would rise, that he would awaken and prove their chief's doubts wrong. They wanted him to be a god, as he had claimed. Others, however, could not bear the thought of such an unnatural being walking among them.

On the third day, Salcedo did not rise. His body remained still, cold to the touch, his chest unmoving. The natives gathered around Urayoán, and there, in the shadows of the rainforest, they came to their conclusion: The Spaniards were not gods. They were men. Fragile, mortal men.

The realization struck like thunder, and in the hearts of the natives, something shifted. Fear turned to anger, and anger turned to defiance. They would no longer worship these strangers who had deceived them. They would no longer bow to these iron-clad invaders.

The revolt came swiftly.

The Spaniards, unprepared for the sudden onslaught, were overwhelmed. The battle was long. A clash of steel and wood, a clash of two worlds at war. The natives fought with the fury of those who had been betrayed, their warriors as fierce as the storms that would ultimately wash away the ships that had been waiting along the shore.

As the Spaniards retreated, the Taíno remembered the lesson that Salcedo had taught them that gods were not made of silver and steel, nor were they pale-faced or blue-eyed devils. They were men like any other, who bled and died under the same sky.

The river of Guaorabo still runs deep, its waters carrying the secrets of those who dared to believe. And though Salcedo is gone, the legacy of his deception lingers like a shadow, a warning etched in the hearts of those who know the true nature of power.

YUIZA

They were called savages. Uncivilized. Lesser than. To the pale faces who arrived at their shores, they were barely even human. But the Taíno people were more than capable of outsmarting, outmaneuvering, and outbattling the invaders who gravely underestimated them. For a time, they held the Europeans back, forcing them to retreat across the sea. It wasn't until those same ships brought over rats, empty promises, corruption, and disease that the pale faces gained the upper hand. Slowly, one by one, each *yucayeque* fell. Territory by territory, the island succumbed to gunpowder, steel, and pestilence.

Despite the many victories of the conquistadors, some strongholds still held firm. Resistance was expected, but they never anticipated it would be led by a woman. Yuiza, one of the few female *caciques* in history, was a force to be reckoned with. Her battle strategy was unparalleled, and her diplomacy was even more impressive. She managed to keep the war at bay, far from her home, hidden in the wilds of Loíza. But even she could not stop the sickness that came with the invaders. No weapon could defeat it, for sickness does not bleed. No walls could contain it, so she had to find another way.

In desperation, Yuiza agreed to a parley with the enemy. She had learned some Latin from missionaries who had visited before. Now, she was ready to make a deal. When Pedro Mejías, a conquistador, met her, Yuiza was surprised. He didn't have the pale skin of the others, but rather, appeared kissed by the sun. Deep down, she believed she could reason with him.

She spoke of how the island and its people were nearly equal in strength, and that the war would never end if they continued. She spoke of the many lives that would be lost. Her people, yes, but his as well. This was a bluff. At one point, it might have been true, but with the sickness at their door, the invaders no longer had the luxury of waiting for a surrender. She hadn't heard from the other settlements in a long while, and she felt alone, with no more cards to play except the fact that these men feared her.

Pedro, caught off guard by her strength and beauty, proposed a deal: if she would marry him and sail with him to Europe as his bride, he would spare her people. It was a strange offer, but it was a proposal of survival. Knowing the strange customs of the Europeans, Yuiza reasoned that their "marriage" was more of a business contract. With no other choice, she agreed to the deal.

When she returned home with the news, her most trusted adviser, Guaitiao, struggled with his doubts but trusted his chief's judgment. Anamoín, Yuiza's close friend and wife to Guaitiao, had reservations. She was pregnant, and she feared for their safety, unwilling to place their future in the hands of a stranger's promises. She begged Yuiza to reconsider, but the decision had been made, and the weight of it was on their chief's shoulders.

Yuiza, their courageous leader, would now live on the shore with Mejías, a wife, a slave with a title, a living sacrifice.

In her absence, the settlement fell into disarray. Mejías wasted no time and sent strange men into the night, who set fires and took whatever they wanted. Guaitiao and his soldiers tried to protect what they could, but they had lost their spirit. Anamoín hid as best as she could, but eventually, she was found. For her defiance, she was beaten, and with a sharp pain to her stomach, she lost her child and her future.

The next morning, the tragedy was known to all. In her grief, Anamoín turned on her old friend, blaming Yuiza for the suffering of their people. She told everyone that their precious chief had made a deal. With her grieving husband at her side, Anamoín reignited the spirit of resistance. She gathered the remaining strength of the people who were fueled by rage with the promise of blood. They marched toward the shore, determined to make Yuiza pay for her betrayal, as well as those who chose to stand with her.

Meanwhile, Yuiza remained in isolation, unaware of what was happening on the island. She had been wrong about marriage, for Pedro sought more than her agreement; he desired to control her body and soul, unchallenged submission. What else had she been wrong about? On a particularly dark day, she looked out from the window of her chamber and saw a mob of furious Taíno emerge from the treeline, marching toward her. They came to rescue their leader, she hoped. But whatever their purpose, it would be loud, and it would destroy whatever fragile peace she had left.

The mob raided the ships, setting the vessels aflame. They stormed Yuiza's quarters, and her fate was sealed. They dragged her from the ship, through the forest, and back to the place she had once ruled. It was in ruins now, and the people she had once led were broken. Anamoín and Guaitiao stepped forward, their eyes filled with judgment, and sentenced Yuiza to death.

Yuiza accepted her fate, standing before the people she had once led. Her decision had been flawed, but it was the only choice she could see in a world that had shifted too far beyond her control. Her heart ached with the weight of the lives lost and the broken promises that had led to this moment. As she stood there awaiting her punishment, she realized that the path she had taken was one of painful compromises, where the line between right and wrong had become blurred. She had chosen life for her people, but at what cost? The blood of the innocent weighed heavily on her conscience, and in the end, it was her people's fury, not her intentions, that had sealed her fate. Yuiza had acted with the belief that her sacrifice, the sacrifice of one, could save the many. But that hope had been shattered by reality.

Her last words, "Forgive me," were not a plea made in fear, but a recognition that sometimes even the best of intentions can be misinterpreted by those who are hurt the most. Her actions would forever brand her not as a savior, but as a symbol of treachery, deception, and death. Despite everything, Yuiza held onto the belief that doing what one truly believes to be right and good, even when the outcome is uncertain or misunderstood, was the only proper path a leader could walk.

"Yunque"- Digital Art From the Coay collection (2024) -

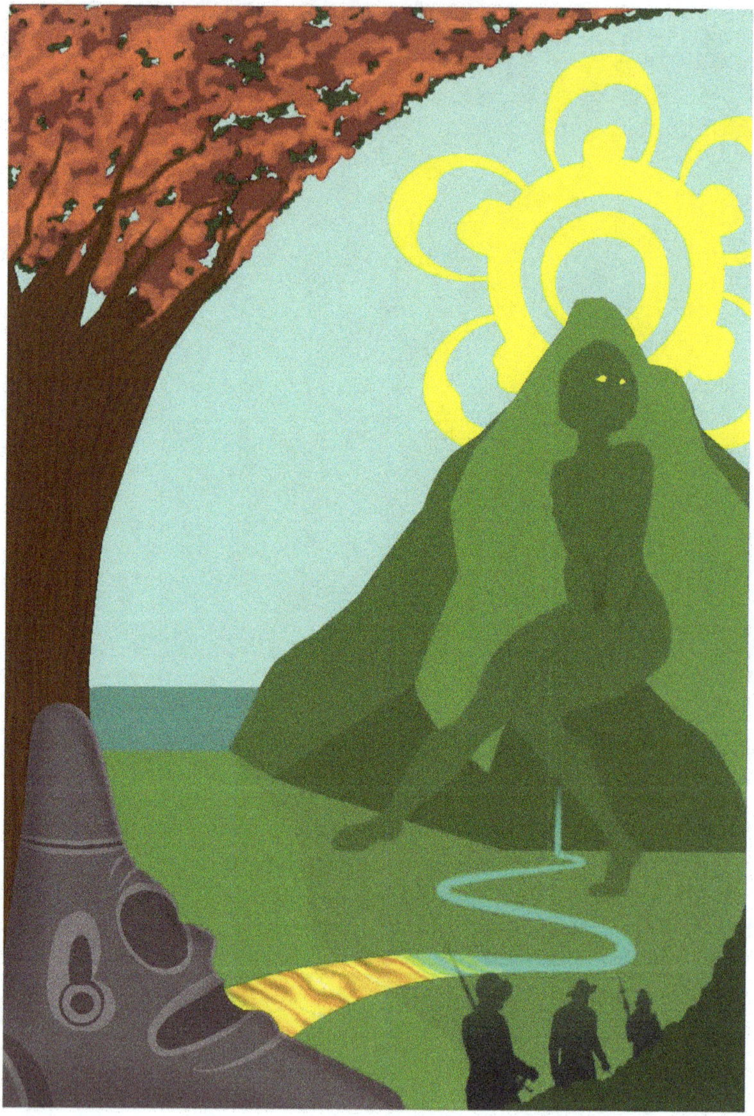

YUNQUE

The Spaniards had been on the island for quite some time. Later, followed by the French, the Dutch, and then all of Europe. Every nation was trying to obtain its piece of the new and bountiful discovery. Every native settlement was ransacked, every Taino enslaved. The island and its natural resources were stripped away, day by day. As the natives worked under European whips relentlessly, the island seemed to lose a certain glow. The birds were hunted down to protect valuable crops. The skies, once painted emerald green with the color of their feathers, were now laid bare, robbed of their beauty and song. The tropical landscape was cut down to make way for stone roads and fortified settlements. What was once a paradise was now a prison and labor camp for those who used to call it home.

A firm "good morning" kick signaled the start of the workday. Tainos would line up at the edge of the river, forced to search for gold through the crystalline ripples, among the pebbles and sand. They scooped up the sludge from the bottom of the bank with bent backs and hand-woven baskets. They then tossed the sludge into the water, washing away everything but a few specks of gold. These minuscule gains of seemingly worthless metal were then collected by the jailers who loomed over the Tainos' working heads.

At a very busy riverbend worked a young girl named Ke. She had never known anything other than this work, so she did her best and never complained. Her entire life was spent sitting in the water, lost in thought, calmly waiting for the river to reveal its treasures. During a shift rearrangement, she caught a glimpse of some new guards arriving at their post. She had never seen them before, and since everything was always the same, she found some pleasantness in these insignificant changes. That pleasantness did not last forever.

The men's eyes briefly met the beauty of Ke, and in their thoughts, they quickly became single-minded. The wolfish soldiers loomed over the unsuspecting girl, rudely interrupting her work and insisting on a private audience. It was only the afternoon, and she didn't speak the language perfectly, so she was confused. Fortunately, Ke could sense that the intention behind their cloudy eyes was not as pure as they made it seem. Though she was often thought of as naïve, she knew enough about these ungracious visitors to understand it was no longer safe. Ke stopped and began to plead with the men to let her continue working, but it fell on deaf ears. The men could not understand her strange words, nor would they have cared. They decided the riverbank was far away enough that no one would hear what they were about to do and began encroaching on her, forcing themselves upon the young girl.

In their haste, they assumed Ke would accept her fate, but it wasn't in the Taino spirit to give up. Her youth and agility, combined with the men's heavy armor, made her quick enough to free herself. She picked a direction and began to run.

In the thicket of the humid forest, Ke found herself lost. The land she once knew had been forever changed by the white men and their parasitic ways. Was she to continue aimlessly into the unknown? She had to. The soldiers followed her, and in the echoes of their voices and gunshots, it was clear they would not relent. Amid the chaos, like a guardian angel, a familiar river appeared to her, flowing freely and unobstructed. Taken as a sign from her gods, she decided to follow the river upstream. She followed it for so long that it was now close to nightfall. She could no longer see the pursuing soldiers, but she could hear them.

Ke followed her heart and the river up a sacred mountain she knew the soldiers had never experienced. She knew that the European invaders would never dare go this high or this deep into this beautiful yet deadly tropical web. Finally, among the waterfalls, the frogs, and the trees, she felt somewhat protected. As she climbed higher and higher, the clouds began to creep into the trees, creating a mysterious curtain that provided much-needed invisibility. Although she sensed the soldiers were no longer on her tail, she could no longer see what was right in front of her. But who needed eyes when the land was actively taking her into its embrace? Ke felt a kind of force, pushing her toward something, a final destination, a haven.

Her intuition had not led her astray yet, so she decided to follow that feeling through the maze of fog.

When she finally emerged from the cloudy embrace of the trees, she found herself in front of a cave-like rock formation. Ke entered and realized that it was not a cave, but a tunnel created by a series of arches and clay walls leading her to the very top of the mountain. When she reached the other side, she found herself slightly above the clouds, with a view that stretched from the treetops and towns to the sand and sea. Ke was overwhelmed and began to cry, seeing the majestic beauty of the island she loved so much.

Deprived of breath and in need of rest after all that running, she decided to go to the eye of the river for a drink. It was the freshest, sweetest, and purest water she had ever had. As some of her salty tears fell into the deep, mirror-like pool, she gave thanks to the great and powerful forces that had saved her. In her blissful happiness, she fell back onto the soft ground, and under the emerging starlight, she fell into a deep and peaceful sleep.

Unfortunately, in her amazement, she had forgotten she was ever in danger and let her guard down. Unlike good-hearted girls, evil does not rest.

Ke was awakened by the soldiers, who used fiery torches and sharpened blades to continue their relentless pursuit. As the stars faded, silence crept back in. Night had come to an end, and the soldiers had gone home fulfilled. The sun rose the next day, expecting to be greeted by Ke's smile, but instead, it was greeted with a most unhappy scene. An innocent girl, who had grown up obedient, knowing nothing but pain and sorrow, had been destroyed by Men and their callous cruelty.

Yucahu looked down upon the girl's tattered and lifeless body, ashamed of himself for abandoning this girl overnight. The mountain top was his throne from which he watched over his people, and yet here one lay, empty. In a rush of duty and compassion, he decided to bestow a gift that would return her life. A life that was so unnecessarily taken away. A life not like the one before, but hopefully one that she could come to accept and enjoy. They would bind her to the island that she so loved.

Her auburn skin began to twist and converge on itself, ascending steadily before branching out. Her blood began to feather and bloom, becoming flowers that nestled on their perch. She became a gorgeous and fiery flamboyant tree, tall enough to gaze over the entirety of the island. Her soul, once trapped within a human vessel, now connected and embodied the mountain and the rainforest that came to be known as El Yunque. Statuesque and powerful, she felt that this was where she was always meant to be.

As punishment for their malevolence, Yunque decided to take away what the colonizers valued most. She focused on the birthplace of all rivers, which she once salted with her tears. The eye began to bubble, then flow. Through the ground and the trees, past the rocks and the leaves, down waterfalls, lakes, and streams, to where slaves searched for what gleamed. The Tainos began to notice the gold dissolve and disappear from their hands. One by one, baskets came back empty. Rivers all across the island seemed drained of their riches. Frantic, the soldiers and countrymen demanded answers and results, but no matter how hard they forced others to work, there was no more treasure to be found.

In fact, the island had been cursed, and there would never be any gold found again. For those who torture and enslave the innocent shall be met with motherly justice. Those who disrespect and abuse nature will not know of her kindness or generosity as long as they live. And so the river, the mountains, and the trees remembered Ke, and the island itself fought back.

Sotomayor y Guanina

Guanina's kisses tasted like honey, and her skin glowed radiant like bronze beneath the island sun. It was no wonder that Cristóbal de Sotomayor fell so deeply in love with her, and with him. Their forbidden love blossomed under the shade of the great ceiba tree, whose thick trunk and twisted roots created a hidden sanctuary from prying eyes. There, their secret meetings could remain untouched by the influence of others. No one knows the exact moment when their hearts entwined, but everyone recalls how it ended. The aching heartbreak caused by a world unwilling to forgive and accept change.

Guanina had been meeting Sotomayor at the sacred tree more and more frequently, and her elder brother, Agüeybaná, began to grow uneasy. Known as El Bravo, he had a reputation for ruthlessness in battle and for being a vicious leader. One afternoon, troubled by her absences, Agüeybaná trailed his sister all the way to the majestic *ceiba*. Between the coiling roots, he saw not just his dear sister, but also the enemy. Fear and confusion gripped him as he watched them exchange a kiss beneath the sprawling tree. Guanina was a traitor, and Sotomayor had stolen her heart. Fury replaced his uncertainty, and Agüeybaná charged forward, his voice thunderous with command. He demanded that Guanina never see Sotomayor again. Desperation painted her face as she cried and pleaded with her brother, but there was nothing either of them could do. Their worlds were as different as night and day, and no one would ever allow their love to exist.

Back home, Agüeybaná spat fire, his words as blunt as his *macana*. "To be with him is treachery," he told his sister. "They are the enemies, all of them monsters who would destroy us if we gave them the chance."

But Guanina assured her brother that Sotomayor was not like the rest. Her love had softened his hatred and drawn out a mercy that she had not seen in any of his kind. Despite her claims, Agüeybaná would not listen and could not understand. He cut her off, refusing to hear her pleas, and warned her one final time.

Back at the camp, Sotomayor's fellow soldiers laughed bitterly at the idea that their leader could fall for one of these wild women. Disgusted, they saw no way in which such a union could survive. But for Guanina and Sotomayor, their affection had already taken root. That very night, as if connected by the force of fate, they both decided to sneak off to the ceiba in hopes of meeting each other. It was serendipity when they found one another, their hearts truly beating as one. Together, they fled toward freedom and independence from the condemning voices. They sought a place where their love could flourish, untainted by war, unbroken by division.

But unfortunately, Agüeybaná's hatred and sense of duty had been underestimated. He woke to find his sister missing, instantly knowing exactly where she had run off to. He recruited a few hunters and headed to the ceiba, where they could track them deeper into the forest. There was no way he would let them escape. It was a race of wills, a tragic game in which the couple could not physically outrun the incoming clan of experienced hunters. Guanina and Sotomayor stopped to rest for a moment, their supplies laid out in the dirt, waiting to continue. At that point, Agüeybaná was closing in and managed to catch up with them. Filled with rage, he confronted Sotomayor.

"You have poisoned my sister's mind. Taken her away from what she knows to be true and right."

Sotomayor, trembling but resolute, denied the accusation, his voice laced with sorrow. He apologized, hoping his words might soften the heart of the brother and warrior standing before him. Agüeybaná would hear none of it. In fact, the pleading only made him angrier. With a growl, he grabbed one of his companions' bows and raised it. With the poisoned arrow ready, he aimed it at Sotomayor and threatened to let it fly.

Guanina stepped forward, her heart breaking at the sight of her brother's fury. "Don't," she begged. "Please, stop this madness."

Sotomayor pushed her out of harm's way, trying to protect her as he accepted his fate. That simple touch was enough for Agüeybaná to let the arrow loose. The moment stretched painfully long. Guanina stumbled in from the sidelines and stood her ground before the man she loved, holding him close. Surprised, Sotomayor instinctively returned the gesture and wrapped his arms around her. At that point, Agüeybaná realized what he had just done.

The arrow flew swiftly through the pair of lovers, the poison striking through their hearts. They fell to the ground, still entwined in each other's arms. Their blood mingled with the earth beneath them.

Agüeybaná, staring down at his sister and her lover, swallowed the bitter taste of grief. His heart was torn by the tragic consequences of his actions, and held no room for tears. In a quiet act of respect for their love that was strong enough to die for, he agreed to bury them together beneath the ceiba. Yet, because Sotomayor was still the enemy, he made sure his body was placed upside down, with his feet sticking out of the earth, so in death he could not find his way to the afterlife. They were to be together under the earth, but separated forever in eternity.

Agüeybaná's heart felt pain and pity for the sister he had accidentally killed. He returned home empty, without family, and with an even bigger thirst for battle. Who knows how the story would have been different if he had been able to see past the haze of doom and difference to understand that we are all capable of goodness? He could have learned that love was one of the greatest weapons against discord and war. But sadly, sometimes the world cannot accept love, no matter how pure. Still, that should not stop one from loving boldly.

La piedra taina

The sun burned brightly over the hills of Guajataca; its rays cast long shadows, much like the ones the Taino people had been reduced to. For Chief Mabodamaca, the last of the Taino *caciques*, it felt as though the dawn brought only a heavy burden. The flames of rebellion had flickered and died time and time again, each revolution proving more futile than the last. His people, once proud and strong, were now broken and defeated by the ever-encroaching Spanish forces. It was as if the very land he loved had grown tired of fighting. Although freedom felt distant, Mabodamaca had one more fight left in him. He whispered it to the winds and gathered men and women who were able and willing to fight. He was able to recruit nearly 600 courageous souls.

Mabodamaca stood at the heart of his people's last stronghold, surrounded by the great warriors, hunters, and gatherers who had chosen to resist the invaders in their new camp. A great speech was given about solidarity and sacrifice. Mabodamaca did not expect it to be an easy victory, but he would make the Spaniards pay dearly for every inch and soul they took. As he spoke, his heart turned to stone in preparation for the future, which seemed as dark as the gathering storm clouds. Afterward, they all retreated to rest for the upcoming battle. As they slept, their breaths synchronized. For some, it would be the last one they'd ever take.

In the dead of night, disaster struck. Under the cover of darkness, the Spaniards arrived, led by a conquistador named Don Diego Salazar. Their numbers were overwhelming, their weapons and tactics ruthless. The Tainos were unprepared for the swift ambush. Salazar's men moved faster than shadows, striking without mercy. The battle raged for hours, and Mabodamaca fought with the ferocity of lightning, defending as many of his people as he could. Unfortunately, when the smoke cleared, all his fighting was in vain. One by one, the Tainos fell, either slain or captured. His people, though brave and skilled, were no match for the might of the Spanish soldiers and their steel uniforms.

Mabodamaca fought until his strength was spent, and his breath came and went in ragged gasps. The chief, bloodied and broken, managed to escape into the thick woods. He was the only one left standing. His heart was empty with the knowledge that his people were now truly lost, their hopes extinguished like the fading embers of a dying fire. Mabodamaca wandered through the forest for days, disoriented and numb. His body ached, and his mind clouded. He had given everything to the cause, but in his head, the question lingered: What was there left to fight for?

The Taino people were no more. Their language, their traditions, and their sacred rituals were all erased. His island, his home, had been conquered. His pride, once unshakable, now wavered.

In the depths of his despair, Mabodamaca made a decision. He would not fall to the Spanish blade or be subjected to the horrors of slavery. If this were to be the end, it would have to be on his own terms. He would be the last to fall, but his fall would be a defiant one, a final statement that the true Taino spirit would never be tamed or oppressed.

And so, Mabodamaca climbed through the dense forest to the edge of a great cliff, his eyes fixed on the land below. The wind howled around him as he stood at the precipice, his body still and resolute despite his injuries. He took a deep breath and let out a mighty battle cry. It was one of defiance that rang through the trees, relinquishing his strength back to the island. The cry died down, and with a simple step forward, he let himself fall.

Mabodamaca's body plummeted through the air like a stone being cast from a great height until he crashed onto the foot of the cliff. The impact shook the earth, and the force of his fall carved an indelible mark in the stone. His face, frozen and colossal, was etched onto the cliffside: a monument that would remain no matter how the world changed. The years passed, and the Spanish continued their conquest. Though the land had changed, though his people had been lost to history, their legacy lived on in the stone. The cacique's face, a reminder that even in defeat, they had left their mark on the world.

To this day, the auspicious face remains, tucked away in the mountains of Isabela, unchanged by time and uneroded by wind and water; a testament as silent as the Tainos' last night of hope and as loud as Mabodamaca's battle cry.

VEJIGANTES

1511- Esteemed General,

I trust this urgent news finds you at a good time. As per your most honorable request, we have followed the noble Juan Ponce de León to the shores of Puerto Rico and, in like manner, have aided in the establishment of further settlements upon the coastline. At great personal cost, I have upended both my family and our lives in pursuit of greater opportunities within this New World. Alas, fate has not been kind, and our expectations have met with struggle.

Two nights ago, our home and caravan were assailed by a small band of the native rebels that still linger in these parts. They took from us provisions, materials, and, most grievously, the festival supplies we had prepared in anticipation of your arrival. A great misfortune indeed, but the events that transpired just yesterday are of even more dire concern. Upon awakening, we were struck with a most disturbing sight. Along the outer bounds of our estate, the savages had taken it upon themselves to craft replicas of our *botarga* masks and had impaled them upon spikes, as if to mock us. Upon closer inspection, it became apparent that these grotesque effigies were no mere imitation, but rather made with a keen craftsmanship, surpassing our own in some respects. They were adorned with what appeared to be human hair and blood, the sight of which has caused my wife to descend into a state of great distress. I fear, as any reasonable man might, for the safety of my household.

It is plain to see that we have underestimated the tenacity of these wild peoples. I cannot help but believe these actions were deliberate threats aimed at driving us from these lands. The noble de León, for his part, remains resolutely indifferent to the matter, dismissing the danger as little more than an inconvenience. Thus, with all due humility, I beseech you for aid in this grievous circumstance. It is beyond doubt that these incidents are but the opening salvo of a far more perilous campaign against us. I shall remain vigilant, and though we are sorely lacking in military assistance, I shall endeavor to hold firm as best I can. Yet, I cannot ignore the pressing need for your intervention in this most troublesome affair. I eagerly await your guidance and hope that swift action will be taken to bring this matter to a timely and safe conclusion.

With the utmost respect,

Your humble servant

1542- My Dearest Love,

I hope this letter finds you well, though I'm sure it will not reach you soon enough. My father insists I stay at home while you are away, and I resent this order with every inch of my young soul. Here, things are not well.

The slaves are causing me no end of discomfort. They've grown even more unruly, especially at night when they gather around their bonfires. They wear repurposed Taino masks now, dancing in them like fools or hanging them on their doors like some kind of warning. Mother says it's because their gods have abandoned them and they're looking for comfort in strange ways. I simply can't comprehend how some ugly, horned monsters could bring someone peace of mind. Then again, there is some sense in it due to the fact or their lack of intellect and class. I can't bear to look out and see those black faces staring back at me, or those awful, hollow eyes that seem to follow me wherever I go. I'm sure they mean no harm, but it's enough to make anyone think they're being cursed.

I've told Father how I feel, and he's cracking his whip as I write, no doubt telling them to cease their pagan tendencies. But the worst part is that I fear they'll blame me for their misfortune, and I'll have to suffer through more of their cold, dead stares. Since you left, I've spent my days doing nothing but waiting and worrying. I won't even leave the house without someone with me now, and I'm sure it's become quite a nuisance. I long for the day when I can leave all this behind and be with you again.

Please, my love, come home soon. I can't bear being away from you any longer, nor will I truly feel safe unless I'm by your side. I miss you more than I can say, and I cannot wait for the day when I can finally be your wife. Till death do us part.

Yours, evermore.

1690- Dear Diary,

Today, I bring good news. For the first time ever, the slaves in this town no longer depend solely on the obedience of the white man to survive. We have gained a bit of freedom to move, though it isn't much. I, who once couldn't read or write, now teach the children how to do so. When I walk down the street, I see more faces of people like me than of the European "master race." It's a good feeling, being able to walk freely, dressed without chains. Just yesterday, I saw a cousin of Ma's running his own fruit cart. He probably won't get many customers with deep pockets, but you can be sure that if one of ours is buying some *quenepas,* we know where we are going.

It's true that we're not completely free yet, but freedom is close. I can taste it in my mouth, like something I've never tried but am certain of its luxurious flavor.

The elders always talk about rebellion, this, rebellion that, but we, the younger, bright-eyed generation, don't want to die fighting before we've even started living. That doesn't mean we don't want to be free. It just seems that taking our machetes to arms might be a dreadful waste of lives. I think one day a time will come when a great battle will have to be fought. Until then, wouldn't it be better to whisper, biding our time until we can scream? Small acts of defiance can go a long way if we have patience.

This week, those first steps have been taken. I've seen young Black people go out at night, covered in rags and pieces of cloth, wearing masks made of coconut and paper, with large horns erupting in every direction. They gather, run through the streets, and if they see a pale face, they smack it rather mockingly with a dried cow bladder. Not enough to cause real pain, but enough to make them angry. We watch them from the shadows, from the windows or alleys, laughing and enjoying the chaos. The guards try to catch them, but the Tricksters are fast and always manage to get away. By dawn, everything calms down. The masters inquire about the monsters, but we know nothing. Even if I did know, I wouldn't tell, and they know that. I guess that's what makes them so mad. The Europeans call them pagan demons or criminals. We have come to call them Vejigantes because of the *vejiga* they carry.

I feel like this is just the beginning; a sign that our misfortunes are soon to end. The first step of defiance that will soon see us free.

Tomorrow, I'll see what happens, but today I go to bed with hope.

Good night.

1858- Greeting, Editors of *La Gazeta de Puerto Rico,*

I am writing to respectfully submit for your consideration a proposed story that I believe would be most worthy of publication in your next issue. Recently, I had the privilege of attending the inaugural festival held in Barrio Playa, Ponce. I am delighted to report that the experience was nothing short of extraordinary. The music, the food, and the people all contributed to what was truly a most memorable occasion. However, it was the pageantry that captivated me above all.

As you are well aware, our island is rich in traditions, and one of the most fascinating is that of the Vejigante, a figure, until now, most often seen during local gatherings. Small towns throughout Puerto Rico craft their own masks and adorn themselves with large tunics and stilts. While this is a familiar spectacle, the occasion I witnessed stood out for the reverence it accorded the monsters we celebrate, elevating them in a manner befitting their significance in our shared history.

The costumes were grand and colorful, some resembling bat wings and serpentine ruffles, while others were an eclectic assortment of shapes and forms. The Vejigante masks themselves displayed an artistry so fine that I would dare say future generations of artisans ought to dedicate themselves solely to this craft, for it is, in its own right, a true form of art. Traditionally, these masks are fashioned from coconut, though many today incorporate papier-mâché and other materials, creating magnificent yet terrifying figures adorned with intricate patterns and vivid hues. While the exact origins of these creatures remain somewhat uncertain, it is evident that they have been influenced by the various cultures that have touched Puerto Rico across the ages.

In conversing with many of the festival's spectators, I gathered that the Vejigantes hold differing meanings for various individuals. To some, they are monstrous embodiments of mankind's darker impulses, a manifestation of evil to be overcome. To others, their sharp teeth and horns mark them as benevolent protectors who serve as guardians to those they consider friends. These figures are both feared and cherished by children, as their stories become an indelible part of their upbringing.

It is for these reasons, dear editors, that I wish to propose a detailed report on these remarkable festivities, so that our traditions may not fade into obscurity but instead be spread throughout the island and beyond. I am certain it is vital for our youth, as well as outsiders, to understand the significance of these figures, the monsters who represent our strength, our tempers, our fear, our quick wit, our music, and our vivid personalities.

I have enclosed a draft of the exposé with this letter and would be most grateful to receive your thoughts on the matter. Should you find my proposal worthy, I would consider it a great honor to assist in preserving this tradition for many years to come.

Sincerely

SIRENA

"Gather around, children, for I have a tale to tell. A story not of man or beast, but of song and ocean, of cursed love and twisted devotion. Only a few know the events and lessons I am about to share, which is why we must pass them on. So listen closely and remember well, because soon, it will be your turn."

"We begin with a Taíno woman named Aycayia, who was undoubtedly the most beautiful in her *yucayeque.* If her looks weren't enough, her voice was said to pierce the veil, a direct link to the heavens. How could something so harmonious and pure not be heard by the gods? Some say she was a helpless maiden, coveted and pursued by every man she met. Others claim she was a promiscuous temptress, bedding other women's husbands - the original scarlet letter. Whatever the case, all eyes were always on her, burning their jealousy, hatred, and distaste directly onto her skin."

"The women soon grew weary and decided they'd had enough. They met in secret, gathered around the fire, to deliberate on their options. Aycayia was to be punished. Their *bohique* had an idea. She suggested they perform a curse, one that could take her far, far away from them, twisting her form into something unnatural and grotesque, something that no one would ever find enchanting again.

They agreed, and cowardly began to chant in ancient Taíno while Aycayia slept. They spoke poetically of the land and sea, of sacrifice and perpetuity. The more they sang, the higher their voices rose. As they reached the crescendo, the flames blew out, and the deed was done."

"Aycayia awoke at that very moment, as though from a nightmare. Sick and thirsty, she stumbled out of her home in the dead of night, searching for water. Her skin felt dry and itchy against the wind, so she scratched at it, and it began to flake off. She made her way to the shore and threw herself into the water. Despite the briny taste, she found the saltwater refreshing. But still, she felt dry. Her nails grew long and sharp as her hunger for hydration grew, and she continued to peel off her skin in chunks. She submerged herself further into the dark embrace of the waves. Amidst the bubbles and algae, she began to shift. Her hair became slimy and silky, her neck grew gills, and her legs fused into a tail with fins. She had become a creature of the sea, a mermaid."

"The *bohique's* curse had worked, but unbeknownst to all the women involved, they had also doomed themselves. The words they spoke to harm and disfigure Aycayia instead turned her into a formidable foe. Her face, once beautiful, was now pearlescent, pristine, and beyond reproach. Her song, now even more powerful, was mesmerizing and hypnotic. Her once short human life stretched into immortality, plenty of time to seek her revenge. And so, Aycayia swam the shores, seducing and terrorizing the women who had cursed her and their husbands."

"Decades passed, and much had changed, both on the island and beneath the waves. The mermaids remained mysterious and untouched below the surface of the water, but Puerto Rico had been conquered. The Taínos were wiped out, and Africans were enslaved. One of those slaves, an elderly African woman, had escaped from her plantation and made it to the shore. She had hoped to swim to one of the smaller islands off the coast, but she was born into slavery and had never learned how to swim. As she struggled in fear, the current quickly pushed her out deeper into the sea. She flapped around helplessly, trying to stay afloat, but eventually, she grew tired, sinking steadily."

"From the cold depths, two pairs of pale hands emerged, holding her delirious body and pushing her back to the surface for air. Still weak and confused, she could barely open her eyes. The strangers whispered softly in her ear, 'Do you wish to be saved?' In her anguish, the old woman managed to whisper, 'Yes,' even though she had no idea who these strangers were, how they had arrived, or what they had planned for her. With her eyes still closed, the two strangers each planted a soft kiss upon her lips."

"When she opened her eyes, she saw that the beings holding her up were not human at all, but merfolk creatures with tails. And, to her shock, she now had a tail as well. Before she could contemplate what was happening to her, the two pale creatures submerged themselves and swam forward, waiting for her to follow. There was no time for fear, for in that moment, all she could think of was her newfound freedom. No one would ever make her a slave again."

"What happened to her after that, no one knows, but the next mermaid sighting wouldn't come until much, much later."

"The island was now booming with tourism, and in a family-run kiosk by the beach, a young teenage fisherman named Ian was about to catch something unexpected. His family's business wasn't doing well they had struggled to stand out from the competition. They had tried to make their *empanadillas* different, using exotic ingredients and even shark meat, but nothing seemed to work. The sea had given all it could, and yet Ian would still get on his little boat and sail out to see what he could catch for the day's menu."

"One afternoon, when the waters were calm and the fish scarce, Ian saw something shimmering beneath the waves. He couldn't tell what it was, but it seemed large and delicious. Determined, he cast his net over his prey and hauled it in. It was heavier than he expected, and when he pulled it aboard, he realized it wasn't a fish at all, but a frightened little merboy."

"Ian approached cautiously, noting the tender, delicate nature of the creature's face. He felt pity. In the creature's eyes, he saw himself lost, naïve, with no idea what to do next. Ian wondered if he should release the merboy or keep him, knowing deep down that keeping him would solve his family's problems."

"He brought the merboy home to ask his family what to do, but he could never have predicted what happened next. As soon as they laid eyes on the creature, they decided to cook it. After all, a magical, mythical creature would surely bring them more business. Ian was horrified at the idea, but his family was insistent; they believed it was their ticket to success."

"Ian's uncle caged the merboy and placed his tail in a basin filled with barely any water. Soon, the merboy let out a bloodcurdling scream, one that Ian felt all the way outside. When Ian checked on the creature, he found that one of its arms was missing, sawed off by his uncle. The wound was poorly bandaged, and the merboy seemed to be crying, humming a melancholic tune. Ian felt deep sorrow, and as their eyes met again, he made a decision."

"He would show mercy."

"Ian grabbed the merboy, placed him in a wheelbarrow, and began to roll him toward the shore, praying his family wouldn't notice. Halfway there, his uncle appeared, grinning and licking his fingers. He saw Ian betraying the family and ran after him. Ian tried to run faster, but with the added weight of the merboy, it was difficult. His uncle caught up to him and grabbed his shoulder. Ian turned to push him away, and in the struggle, the spear gun went off, striking his uncle in the chest."

"As the body fell to the ground, Ian couldn't believe what had just happened. He knew his life would never be the same. He would either end up in prison or be forced to live on the run. But he knew if he could do one last good deed, it would be for the merboy. So, he kept going, dumping the merboy into the water."

"Ian looked back and saw his family frantically gathered around his uncle's body. *What now?* He thought. The merboy tugged at his pant leg and urged him into the water. With nothing left to lose, Ian followed. Once they were deep enough where they couldn't touch the seafloor, the merboy kissed Ian and pulled him under. Neither of them was ever seen again."

"Mermaids were once again forgotten until word of the mysterious 'Sirenita de Isla Verde' reached the ears of marine biologist Santiago Rivera. Intrigued by the rumors of merfolk, he began to investigate. Every night, he heard a haunting melody carried by the wind, which only made him more curious. He went to the shore with deep-sea microphones, hoping to record these strange sounds and uncover their source."

"After several failed attempts, Santiago recorded a very clear track. He studied it obsessively, and soon, he couldn't stop replaying the song. He was captivated, almost in love with it, and determined to find its source."

"The next night, he played the recording on a speaker underwater, hoping to lure the creature to him. It didn't take long for her to appear, gently ascending from the waves, glowing in the moonlight. He was mesmerized by her beauty, enhanced by the mystery that surrounded her. As she neared, he bent down to meet her. She caressed his face, as if enjoying the view."

"Without saying a word, she led him into the water. When they reached a deeper part, she broke the silence, offering to show him the wonders of the deep. As a marine biologist, he was intrigued and, selfishly, he wanted to spend more time with her. He agreed."

"She kissed him, a kiss so magical that he felt it in every fiber of his being. When she pulled away, he realized he could no longer feel his legs, but his vision had sharpened. As a smart man, he understood what had happened, but it was too late. She took his hand, and together they descended into the depths."

"Santiago, at peace, now understood: what could the land above provide him that the ocean could not? His new life would be full of discovery, magic, and love. What more could he want?"

"They too disappeared into the water, leaving everyone to wonder whether having a tail was truly a punishment or, in fact, a blessing. The curse of the sea's kiss is still holding strong to this day, waiting for the next human to fall under its weight."

"So, children, now you know some of our forgotten ocean tales and the important lessons they teach us. Be it a woman's vengeance or mercy, a mermaid's kiss, or a siren's song, there is beauty and brutality within everything, a balance that must be respected. As you pass these stories on, remember to stay true to who you are and never fear the unknown that comes with change and growth."

Cofresí

To Whom It May Concern,

I, Roberto Cofresí, bestow upon the finder of this letter my side of the story. I stand in this cold, damp cell beneath El Morro, moments away from death. I see the guards from my small window, preparing for my execution with smiles upon their faces, glad to be rid of the menace that is me. My final wish is that at least one soul knows the truth of my life. So much has been said about me from protected corners and padded palaces, both good and bad. They call me a pirate, which I am, but they paint me as the villain, unworthy, unjust, and crooked. I know for a fact, however, that I am none of those things. I will not die without defending my slandered name, which brings me to my humble beginnings.

As a boy in Rincón, I suffered under egregious conditions of poverty that struck hardworking families the hardest. We all tried our best to make ends meet. We were diligent, obedient, and loyal, yet it was never enough. Most days, my mother wasn't able to feed us. Our father often went without work, so by a young age, I built a great distrust for the system the Spanish king had implemented. I learned my way around a coin, how to hustle and cheat, using my charisma and intellect. But it was never enough, not for my family's security or anyone else's, for that matter. So, the time finally came when the ocean called me, and I answered. Can you blame me? I was left with no choice and became a sailor and then a pirate. I managed to rustle up a crew and steal a ship, which I named "La Anna" after my sister. I began my plundering, and by God, I was good at it.

I would never sail too far from the island, raiding ships traveling to and from Puerto Rican shores. My people needed me, and I wasn't going to forsake them like the Spanish rule did. Despite what one might think of my dangerous and illegal profession, I had a code of honor. Unlike many pirates, who engaged in the typical ruthless violence, I preferred to show mercy, give back, and do things precisely for the right reasons. I chose to lead by extending a helping hand rather than by fear. I would only raid bountiful Spanish merchant ships in hopes of weakening their hold over us. The loot I acquired was not hoarded but put to good use. I am the type of man who shared my wealth with my crew and islanders alike, which helped me earn and maintain their loyalty, respect, and admiration.

By no fault of my own, I quickly became a celebrated symbol of defiance against colonial rule. Unfortunately, all the noise I was making attracted the attention of the authorities, which pressured the Puerto Rican government to hunt me down. They had no interest at first, but as we all know, when the crown calls upon you, you answer.

I was soon betrayed and captured, though I hold no one but those in power responsible. I was put on trial and unjustly found guilty of piracy, among other "crimes." My death sentence was all but certain, and the method of choice; firing squad. I tried my best to be just and honorable and give back as much as I did, but it didn't work. I can now only hope that, at only 34 years of age, I have been able to create ripples of change.

If my execution weren't enough, these idiots tried interrogating me about the large treasure they believe I've hidden somewhere on the island. Despite being tortured, I never yielded and let them know there was no such treasure. They didn't believe me, which makes sense since I've never been a very good liar. You know what I say? Let them search high and low, because they will never find the treasure they seek. Let them fall into madness, struggling under their greed. I will say this, however: The one who inevitably finds my hidden bounty better be pure of heart, or they risk losing their soul.

Thank you for listening to my ranting, stranger. Now that I've passed along my story, I can go in peace. They'll be coming for me soon, but I take joy in death knowing that my life, albeit short, was full of intrigue, adventure, and purpose. The names of the soldiers who take my life today will be forgotten sooner than the change in tide, while I will be remembered in perpetuity. I will have a lasting legacy, not as a criminal, but as a hero.

Sincerely,

The Infamous and Notorious Pirata Cofresí.

EL PUENTE

Angel, a middle-aged single-minded *hacendado*, had a wife and two daughters whom he cared for deeply. As the breadwinner, responsible for providing, he was in charge of the money, but there was one thing that often led him astray: his love for drinking. A hard day's work was often followed by him spending most of his earnings, drowning in liquor and libations.

One evening, after a particularly grueling day of labor, Angel found himself intoxicated and caught up in a gamble. He bet on a fight, convinced he'd win, but in the end, he lost everything. When he laughed and claimed he couldn't pay, the men whom he owed money grew furious. They beat him, leaving him bruised, and threatened him with worse to come. If he didn't pay up, they would take his house—and his wife.

Returning home on horseback, battered and hungover, Angel was greeted by his wife. When she asked what had happened, he explained his predicament. She listened in silence, her face a mask of sadness. This man who stood before her was no longer the same one she had fallen in love with all those years ago. There was no time to dwell on their misfortune, for their safety was at stake. She straightened her back and made a plan. They had to pay the debt quickly or their family would be in danger.

Without hesitation, she had the house stripped of everything that could be sold, and the family began rationing food. They cut corners wherever possible, until they had saved enough to pay the men. Angel took the money to settle the debt, and their troubles were now behind them. As he was leaving, he overheard a conversation between some other men. They were talking about a new fight, one that could get him and his family out of the hole he had dug for them. Hope flared briefly in his chest, but as the reality set in, he realized they were nearly destitute. They had nothing left. There was no way he could place a bet, not even if he wanted to.

The crushing disappointment reignited the desire to drink. As soon as he got home, with nothing left to lose, Angel pulled out his flask and began to drown himself in the drink, trying to numb the overwhelming weight of his choices. His daughters were unaware of the full extent of their family's situation, but it was somewhat obvious that they were destitute, and it became clear to them that their parents needed help. The girls had been saving a small amount of money for new shoes because they were old and riddled with holes. Nevertheless, they wanted to help in any little way they could. They approached their father, offering him their savings, the last of their small stash, to help with getting the family back on track. Angel gladly took the money and left the house with it, but in his drunken state, instead of buying food or anything practical, Angel saw an opportunity to gamble once more. He could erase all the damage he had caused; if only he won.

The road to the fight was familiar: hills, dirt paths, and the bridge that crossed the river. He had traveled this way countless times, but tonight, something felt different. It all seemed a bit more eerie and unsettling than usual. As he neared the bridge, he began to hear strange noises in the distance. Some locals had said they'd heard a strange thing on the bridge before, but Angel had never taken those rumors seriously.

As he got closer, the sounds grew louder. To his horror, he realized they were the erratic cries of a baby. Alarmed, he dismounted and looked around, but between his blurry vision and loss of balance, he barely moved. The cries continued, growing more frantic. Finally, he spotted something at the center of the bridge: a baby, loosely swaddled, crying desperately. Angel approached cautiously, wondering who could have left the child here. The baby looked healthy, but something felt wrong. He gently caressed the baby's face and said, "Let's get you into town. Someone there will know what to do with you."

As he looked down at the baby, its smile twisted unnaturally. The baby's eyes darkened, and it began to laugh widely, revealing a full set of sharp, grotesque teeth.

Angel froze for a second in utter disbelief, giving the baby time to bite into his finger, severing it in one swift motion. He screamed in pain, stumbling back, clutching the bleeding stump on his hand. The shock of the movement startled his horse, which bolted away into town.

In the eerie silence, the baby continued to laugh, now covered in blood, before speaking in a voice far too mature and robust for its tiny frame.

"Well, well, if it isn't my Angel. You've made me so proud. Of all my projects, you are among my favorites. No matter the blessings you receive or the prayers you've had granted, it is so easy to tempt you. You've fallen so far, and it brings me such joy to watch you destroy yourself. Even now, you betray your sweet, generous, and kind daughters. You're going to waste their money.

Angel, dazed and confused, managed to croak, "Who…what are you?"

The baby's smile stretched wider, teeth bared. "You ask, but you already know. I am the one who visits you in your dreams. I make sure your bottles are always full. I am the king of darkness, the prince of lies, fallen from heaven; the devil in disguise."

"Why…why?" Angel asked, his voice weak and filled with disbelief.

"Why you?" the baby continued, its voice growing colder.

"Because you make it easy. You're weak. Why here? Because I enjoy the view. Why me? Because I enjoy seeing the faces you all make. Very entertaining. But enough about me, this is about you. You have places to be. This talk has gone on long enough. We'll meet again… in Hell."

And as quickly as it had appeared, the horrific creature vanished, leaving Angel wide-eyed and trembling with disbelief. He spent hours on the bridge, lost in thought as the sun moved across the sky. He had no idea how much time had passed. After what felt like an eternity of self-reflection, Angel slowly stood up, his mind clearer than it had been in years. The encounter had sobered him. Instead of heading to the town, he turned around and made his way home. When he arrived, his wife awaited him. Angel first returned the money to his daughters, embracing them tightly. He asked for their forgiveness, promising that he would do better from then on. He then kissed his wife and vowed to live actively and with purpose, not dragging himself through life by a noose of his own making.

He found this to be true; that sometimes, it takes a single moment to change. We must embrace each experience as an opportunity to learn, to choose the light.

GARITA DEL DIABLO

"Para España...

Para mi padre...

Para Diana..."

That was Sanchez's mantra. He would often recite it to himself, sometimes to seek courage and sometimes to remind himself of the reasons why. Since he was a boy, his father had instilled in him a deep sense of duty and pride toward his family and their country. Expertly molded by his father's influence, Sanchez grew into the image of a perfect son—someone any parent would be proud of. While this smothering shaped him into an ideal heir, it also left Sanchez insecure, obtuse, and desperate for approval.

Had it not been for a local *mulata* girl named Diana who caught his eye, one might assume Sanchez had no will of his own. A small courtship followed between the enamored youths, one that eventually led to talk of marriage. They would often sneak off to the countryside, where he would serenade her with his mandolin. Even though it was only a hobby for Sanchez, Diana would encourage him to lean more into his music since it was something he loved to do. They supported each other in every endeavor and dreamed of a life beyond what they both knew. To their dismay, neither family was particularly fond of the union. Sanchez's father, in particular, took a keen interest in the time the couple spent together. Though he wished for his son to be happily married someday, he viewed Diana as a distraction. He envisioned a future for his son that a young woman's affection could only derail. With a few carefully pulled strings, Sanchez's future was sealed. The next day, he was sent off to a training camp to become a soldier, and in the future, a general.

In his hopelessness, Sanchez knew that the only thing he could do was distract himself from the loss of the one thing he ever truly desired. So, he focused on becoming a great military man. Perhaps one day, when his father's pride no longer loomed over him, Diana could be his.

The training went well, albeit at a mediocre pace. Sanchez was soon assigned to the greatest fortification in the New World, the San Cristobal Castle. His lack of natural talent and charm did little to help him earn respect from his fellow soldiers. Everyone at the fort had earned their place, but Sanchez had skipped the line, and that fact was not well-received. He quickly became the fort's designated punching bag, bullied by many of his peers. He was perpetually stuck with the worst assignments, including night duty at the most isolated and haunted sentry post in the entire fort.

The sentry post was so remote that soldiers had reported hearing strange noises and seeing ominous shadows in the night. Some came to call the post La

Garita del Diablo. While Sanchez did not believe in such things, he could not deny the many strange occurrences he had witnessed. It was customary for those on duty to shout out, ensuring that their comrades remained awake and vigilant, an informal game to break the monotony of staring into the vast emptiness of the night.

It was well-known that women were not permitted in the barracks, yet one day, Diana managed to sneak in to visit her lover, bringing him sweets and comfort. Despite his father's hopes that a life of service would be enough to fulfill Sanchez, the young couple's affection endured and found a way. However, this visit did not go unnoticed. As punishment for breaking the rules, Sanchez was ordered to remain at his post for three days and nights without relief. He reluctantly accepted the punishment and set off for his new prison, armed only with some rations, his rifle, and a mandolin.

For three long days, he suffered. He passed the time by staring out over the vast blue ocean or repeating a tune on his mandolin as he sang: "Para España... Para mi padre... Para Diana..." When his turn came to call out on the first night, Sanchez's voice was low and distant. The second night, his voice was barely audible. On the third and final night, there was no sound at all. The other soldiers on duty were curious and concerned. Eventually, they concluded that he must have fallen asleep. They deemed it a fitting fate for someone so unprofessional and privileged.

The next morning, a group of soldiers, along with the general, made their way to the sentry post to relieve Sanchez and reprimand him for falling asleep on the job.

When they opened the gate, they were met with a chilling sight: Sanchez was nowhere to be found. All that remained was his empty rifle, a broken mandolin, and his discarded uniform on the floor. They searched the area, but there was no trace of the poor man. No one could explain what had happened.

Speculation ran wild. Some believed that Sanchez had deserted his post, somehow sneaking out of the fort to meet Diana and run away together. Others thought that he was overwhelmed by his miserable treatment and the solitude, and decided to take his own life by casting himself into the sea. Most, however, believed the most obvious explanation: his melancholic singing had summoned the devil, who had taken him away.

No one really knew what happened, but the legend endured. From that day forward, the sentry post was feared and avoided, forever known as La Garita del Diablo. Even today, the area remains haunted, and no one is permitted to approach. But should anyone dare to venture near, they might just hear the soft, haunting melody of a mandolin, still playing for Diana.

MANATÍ

From the tempered skies of the great European nations to the sweltering, sun-scorched heart of a colonial paradise, many families made the trip to try their fortunes in strange lands. The Brasa family had traveled far. Upon their arrival in San Juan, they were given land by the sea. The land was a stretch of unpolished acres, waiting for the hand of man to shape it. A newly constructed house stood at its center, welcoming them to their *hacienda*. Within the house, there was a staff to command, as was the way of the colonies. The Brasa family, having exhausted almost all of their modest fortune, was determined to make the most of this new adventure.

With the air of salt in their lungs and the sound of the waves in their ears, they planted coffee, tobacco, and sugarcane. The fields grew tall under their care, and the crops swayed like offerings to god. They built an empire, one rooted in blood, sweat, and the weight of family history, both at home and abroad. The common dynamic between slaves and their masters was the backbone of the day-to-day operation of the property.

The Brasa family, although not extraordinarily generous or respectful, was far more forgiving and patient than many others. There were many worse places a slave could be. Among them was a slave girl named Ayoka, who counted herself among the lucky ones. She grew up alongside the family's sons and became friends with the youngest, Alfonso. While his brothers spent their time playing and awaiting the day they could leave home and become men, Alfonso spent his days working the land with his father and his afternoons with Ayoka, having all kinds of fantastical adventures among the crops and weeds. As they grew older, friendship turned into more, and from one moment to the next, their lives became much more complicated, filled with deception and a constant need to look over their shoulders.

After Señor Brasa's passing, the young man was gifted the estate in recognition of his hard work and dedication to the family and their land. Alfonso was now not only responsible for the *hacienda* but also retained ownership of all the slaves who worked under his family's name. But how could he give himself completely to his family's legacy if his heart belonged to a slave? Alfonso saw in her a past that they had shared and a reflection of who he longed to be. They experienced life differently. Alfonso, who lived a life of relative privilege but would risk it all for love, and Ayoka, whose life had been shaped by hardship and the heavy chains of history, took a chance on something unexpected. Together, they whispered promises of a life in peace and as equals, a fiction they tried to manifest for themselves.

As most secrets do, theirs soon came to light after an unexpected visit from his older brothers. Before returning home, they had stopped by an improvised canteen where they served crude rum. There, they heard an unsettling rumor. Among the men present, there was talk of a crime committed by none other than Alfonso.

The brothers could not believe it, so they interjected with curious concern. There had been rumblings that he had fallen for one of his slave girls and had been seen proudly expressing their familiarity. Although it was common to take an African woman as a lover, one was never supposed to fall in love; it was a deeply unspoken rule among men. Determined to clear things up and talk some sense into Alfonso, his older brothers suggested they march up to the house to get to the bottom of it. Unfortunately, while they had been living in high society, they had forgotten the ways of the wild white man. One does not add kindling to a liquor-soaked flame. In their drunken state, they took to the streets with torches and rifles in hand. Whatever they had just started, it was certainly not good.

That same night, Alfonso was returning from some business, expecting to greet his love as he made it home. But something wasn't quite right. There was a faint smell of something burning and a gentle yet persistent galloping sound in the distance. As he looked back toward the road, he saw them: torches flickering in the fading light, the determined grunts of angry men. He knew why they were heading this way. They had come for him, for his Ayoka.

He ran to the house, his heart racing, the world a blur around him. Ayoka was inside, cooking their evening meal. She looked up at him, confusion on her face. He didn't need to speak; her eyes caught the terror in his. She knew.

Hearing the sounds of guns and horses approaching, they fled out the back door, maneuvering to

71

avoid being seen. Alfonso and Ayoka sprinted into the night, pursued by a man on horseback. Alfonso grabbed Ayoka and told her to run and hide somewhere safe. Once she saw her chance, she was to get to the beach, where they could take a boat out to sea, far away from this terrible reality. Ayoka's eyes met his, and for the briefest moment, there was understanding between them, a silent vow that, no matter what, they would find each other again. She kissed him, then let go, disappearing into the trees. Alfonso, now solely focused on the man on horseback, drew his pistol and shot to kill.

Alfonso reached the beach first, breathless and wild-eyed. He turned back to see his family home burning. The flames licked the sky, their glow casting long, foreboding shadows. In the distance, the men shouted, the gallop of their horses thundering in pursuit. He could see them drawing nearer, which meant he had to hide. He searched for the boat he had planned to escape with, only to find it already sabotaged and set aflame, the bright fingers curling up and pointing to the night sky. His heart sank, but there was no time to mourn, no time for hesitation. He jumped into the cold night water and awaited a miracle.

As the barbarous men reached the beach, they began to scan the perimeter for signs of life. Unsafe and on the brink of discovery, Alfonso could only think of Ayoka. His stomach twisted with the knowledge that she was out there somewhere, alone, running for her life. As the men's eyelines closed in on his hiding place, Alfonso had no choice. With one final glance at the burning remains of his life, he turned to the water and pulled himself under into the ocean's eternal embrace.

The moonlight kissed the water, and it felt strangely quiet under the waves. The cold water closed over him, the salt stinging his skin as he swam further out, hoping the darkness would hide him. His lungs burned as he held his breath, the sound of the men overwhelmed by the silence of the sea. Could this work? Would Ayoka be waiting, safe and sound, when he returned to shore?

Alfonso did not know how long he could stay underwater. His chest tightened, his body screaming for air, for warmth. To surface was to be discovered and killed. To stay submerged was to die. Steadfast, Alfonso decided he would rather go out on his own terms than fall at the hands of those brutes. As he choked on the saltwater, the world around him began to fade to black. The moon watched from above, its light soft and distant. In that moment, something miraculous happened. The waves whispered with tenderness, and they reached down into the depths and took Alfonso with them. A family of manatees revealed themselves from the deep nothing and escorted him to a shelter of transformation.

The men, tired with their torches extinguished and their anger spent, headed home. As the night began to fade, the fires died, and the smoke settled. Ayoka reappeared. She emerged from the woods, walking slowly, her heart full of dread and hope in equal measure. She made her way to the beach where they had promised to meet. But what was left of the boat was cinder, and there was no sign of the man she had expected to be waiting.

Ayoka stood at the water's edge, staring out into the waves. Had he left her? Was he dead? She knew him too well, and their love was true; he would never leave her. Somehow, she knew he was out there, beneath the water, alive yet unreachable. Their lips were never to touch, their eyes never to meet. Her tears slipped from her face and mingled with the salt of the sea. She did not sleep that night, nor the next. She stood on the shore, stuck in the same spot. As she gazed out to the lonely horizon, her feet began to sprout roots, twisting outward and down past the water and into the sand. She was now rooted in place, immovable. Time continued to slip away. Her hair grew wild and tangled with the salty winds, her arms stretched upward like branches, and she began to catch on her hair, which in turn began to sprout leaves. The dry air and relentless sun ravaged her clothes until there was nothing left, leaving her skin to dry and harden like bark. By the time she stopped crying, her tears had turned the water thick and briny. And there she would remain, multiplying, growing, waiting.

As for Alfonso, he did return, but he was not the same as he was. The ocean had claimed him, and in its depths, he was now something new and of the water: a creature of peace, love, and grace. A smooth-skinned, wide-eyed manatee who would wander forever. He expected to find his love still waiting on the shore, or at least moved on to have a happy life, but all he found was a mangrove tree that vaguely resembled her.

Swimming further in, he sampled the brine. The taste unlocked familiarity. Alfonso realized he wasn't the only one who had undergone a metamorphosis. Both saved yet doomed, inches apart yet so far away.

And so, the manatees roam the shores of Puerto Rico, slow and innocent, creatures of the sea and the salt. Their eyes are full of the sorrow of lost love. Constantly drawn back to the mangrove forests they consider home.

CALLE DEL CRISTO

I first heard the story of the miracle on Cristo
Street from my *abuelo* when I was just a boy. He used to
tell it on quiet evenings when the night was clear and the
moon shone proud. It wasn't a tale you'd find in history
books or adapted to the silver screen, but it was a story
that stuck with me. It was about a man, a horse, and a race
that no one would soon forget.

Baltazar Montañez was something of a local
legend in old San Juan. He wasn't a man who went
around looking for fame, yet everyone knew his name. He
was a jockey, and not just any jockey, but one of the best
Puerto Rico had ever seen. His horse was a beauty: ghost
white, with a mane that shimmered like silver. Her name
was Luna. Together, they were unstoppable.

It was derby season on the island, and many
foreign representatives and talented equestrians were
arriving by boat for the events. One night, a foreigner
named Benoit came to stay at the same inn as Baltazar. He
was polished, with an air of arrogance about him. After
some drinks and hearing incessant praise about their star
jockey, he challenged Baltazar to a race. He claimed that
now that he had arrived, it was Benoit who deserved their
praise.

From quiet curiosity to a bustling, crowded altercation, they spoke of horses, of speed, of agility, of which steed could claim the title of best on the island. Baltazar wasn't the kind to normally take offense at this kind of slander, but the entire island was being questioned, and when it comes to his people, this kind of talk was unacceptable. The challenge was laid out: an illegal race through the streets of Old San Juan under the cover of night, during a time when only the stars could judge them.

Soon enough, the streets were cleared of eager spectators, and boatmen took their mark. Baltazar's heart burned with the people's pride, beating in unison with Luna's. Benoit's horse was a sleek European stallion, but not even that could intimidate the great Montañez. The moonlight bathed the streets in glistening majesty, casting shadows against the walls of the buildings that lined them. The *adoquines,* made from ashy blues, looked black in the gentle glow. These stones were part of the land itself. They had seen battles, celebrations, and countless stories unfold. That night, they would witness something no less legendary.

The race began with a sudden flick of a handkerchief. The horses' hooves struck the *adoquines* and created sharp echoes that tore down the path in front of them. The air was tense with excitement, and in the canopy of buildings, a crowd watched from their windows with bated breath. The thundering of the horses was almost deafening as they raced neck and neck, pushing each other for the lead. Luna seemed to glide rather than gallop, her movements smooth as a breeze. In contrast,

Benoit's mount thundered forward, each stride driven by brute force and determination.

The race brought them down a straight stretch of Calle del Cristo. Perhaps by fate or chance, Benoit's horse pulled ahead. Baltazar's heart sank at the faraway thought of losing, so he urged Luna forward. The pressure built. Sweat coated the back of his neck. His hands gripped the reins tightly. The road ahead seemed endless, stretching further as they rode along. In their defiance of fate, both rider and steed found a hurried trove of passion. Their breathing synchronized as they put their goal into focus. With the steady drumming of her hooves, Luna was able to close the gap. Her legs seemed to work faster than ever before, the beautiful buildings and spectators a blur as they rushed past. They would surely win.

All roads must end, and so did Calle del Cristo, which only led to a great drop off the fort wall. They were both supposed to turn left onto Calle de la Fortaleza when Baltazar came to a realization: Luna was moving faster than he could control. In the distance, the sound of the onlookers' cheers died out. The sharp neighs and pounding hooves spooked some pigeons resting nearby, sending them into the air with frantic wings. They flew right into the unsuspecting Baltazar, momentarily obscuring his sight. The drop ahead loomed large, and it was too late to stop. Luna continued off the edge as if taking flight, their shadow briefly aligning with the moon.

Horse and rider had disappeared into the night. Those who had been watching began to exit their homes and gather at the site of the fall. They leaned over the edge, expecting to see something morbid and tragic, but from the silence and tears came whispers. Baltazar and Luna were nowhere to be found. No corpses, no blood, only the sad truth that nobody could have survived a fall like that. The morose public returned to their beds. In the wake of the tragedy, Benoit's victory was ignored, though he proudly accepted his win at the finish line.

The next morning, something incredible happened. Just as the sun crept over the horizon, Baltazar and Luna appeared, walking back into the city as if nothing had happened. Horse and rider showed no sign of injury, no sign of the fall. People gathered once more, staring in disbelief. How could anyone survive a fall from such a height? How could they have survived the night? Logical reasoning had no answer, for that is not how the world works. The droves of people went to greet him and asked him to explain, but he could not. It was as if he didn't even remember what had happened. He continued home with Luna, leaving people to wonder and speculate.

And so they did. The people of San Juan knew what they had seen, and they came to the conclusion that they had witnessed a miracle. Soon enough, rumors spread of the legend of Baltazar Montañez and the unbelievable events of that night. Stories of the race, the horse and rider's tragic fall, and impossible return became part of the old city's charm.

In the years that followed, as the legend was ingrained not only in the people but in the site of the incident, the citizens of the capital soon decided to honor what had happened. They built a chapel on the very spot where Baltazar had fallen. The chapel was named Capilla del Cristo, after the saint of healing and health, credited with saving Baltazar and Luna's lives. It became a symbol of sorts, where people came to witness, remember, and occasionally feed the pigeons.

A mystery that has forever remained unanswered was eventually branded as folklore. When you walk through the streets of Old San Juan, you can still visit Capilla del Cristo. The chapel stands as proudly as it did all those years ago, watching over the city with droves of greedy fowl perched on its façade. And sometimes, if you listen closely, especially at night, you might hear the clip-clop of Luna's hooves.

It's strange, you know. Some say that miracles only happen to the chosen or the worthy, less often than not. But maybe, if we take a moment to stop, to pay attention, we'll see that they happen all around us, even in the most unlikely of places.

AZUCAR

The sugar plantations were alive with activity. The humans worked tirelessly, hacking down the tall sugar cane and hauling it to the mills, where massive machines would grind it all into a fibrous pulp. The turning and pressing of the cogs released what they called *guarapo*, a syrupy nectar, cloudy and sweet, irresistible in its purest form. It was a treat like no other, bestowed upon the earth by nature itself.

Despite not being part of the usual diet, animals of every kind gathered around the mill, eager to lick up the remnants of the sugary mess left behind by the human workers. Once the barrels were full, the humans would take the *guarapo* to be refined, leaving the mill unattended and ready to be feasted upon. Busy with their work and focused only on profits, the humans saw the animals as pests to be removed. The creatures had to go, but the men couldn't afford to waste time chasing them down. So, a solution was proposed, one that was natural and effective.

They brought in a *guaraguao*, a mighty falcon, whose sharp eyes could spot any creature from miles away. With its powerful wings and piercing talons, it claimed dominion over the mill and the surrounding fields. The great bird would swoop down and eat anything that moved, driving the other animals away. As long as the falcon circled above, no animal dared venture near the sweet syrup. The *guarapo* would go to waste, and the creatures would leave, leaving the mill in peace. Most of the animals, over time, grew tired of the danger and the waiting, so they returned to the safety of the forest. But three persistent friends, an old wild boar, a tiny field mouse, and a sprightly reinita bird, could not resist the allure of the sugary treasure. They waited in the shadows of the tree line, biding their time.

On a hot summer's day, a small pitirre, an unassuming gray bird, moved into the mill. It made its nest in a corner of the man-made structure, unbothered and content. The three friends were surprised to see such a brave newcomer and wondered if he knew of the dangers that lurked above. From the safety of a bush, they called out to him cautiously.

"Don't you fear the guaraguao?" asked the boar, his voice low.

The pitirre chuckled, fluffing his feathers. "This is my home now. I've claimed it. Any creature who is respectful is welcome here."

The three friends exchanged uncertain glances but decided to give it a try. They emerged from the underbrush, moving toward the mill with cautious hope. To their astonishment, no falcon appeared. No claws descended upon them. They drank deeply from the syrupy remnants, their thirst quenched and their bellies full. Days passed, and the new peace held. The friends returned every day, growing bolder with each visit. They revelled in the sweetness, basking in the warmth of the sun. But, as with all good things, their newfound security was soon to be compromised.

One afternoon, when the pitirre was away, the three friends approached the mill once more. They had never known the pitirre to leave, so they never thought to check. As they neared, a shadow darkened the ground. The guaraguao stood before them and blocked their way like the self-righteous falcon that he was.

"You!" the falcon sneered, eyeing them with disdain. "Did you all really not learn your lesson? I'll admit that I've been neglecting my duties here, but I won't make that mistake again. So, who's on the menu?"

The boar quickly bolted back into the treeline in fear. The reinita fluttered away with a frightened tweet. The mouse, however, being too small and not fast enough, was trapped in the guaraguao's clutches. Under the weight of the falcon's talons, he squealed in terror. His friends watched helplessly from the safety of the bush, feeling terrible for leaving their friend behind.

Just then, a blur of gray shot from the sky like a bullet. The pitirre, who had returned just in time, swooped down, slamming into the guaraguao with the force of a cannonball. The falcon stumbled, surprised by the tiny bird's boldness.

"This is my territory. *My* home. You are not welcome," the pitirre declared with fierce confidence, his tiny chest puffed out.

The guaraguao, momentarily stunned, gathered himself and let out a low, mocking laugh. "Your territory? Look at yourself. You think you can stop me?" With a screech, he lunged at the pitirre, wings spread wide, talons bared, ready to strike. The pitirre was quick. He darted and twisted, weaving through the air with incredible agility. The guaraguao, though larger and more powerful, was slow and clumsy in comparison. The battle raged above the mill, a spectacle of feathers and speed. The animals below watched in awe, not believing their eyes. The tiny pitirre, once thought weak, was striking the guaraguao repeatedly without fail. It was a true David and Goliath moment, and like David, the tiny pitirre should not have been underestimated.

The guaraguao grew frustrated by the pummeling and the relentless pecks. Forgetting his ego and tremendous pride, he fled, stumbling as his wings flapped. The guaraguao had been embarrassed, defeated, and was never seen again.

Below, the animals cheered. The little pitirre had done the impossible. The smallest bird had driven away the fiercest predator.

From that day on, the creatures were able to come back to the mill, no longer afraid. They came and went freely, their bellies full of sweet *guarapo*, in a peaceful rhythm that had been missing but had now returned. The pitirre, who had once been thought of as small, now stood proudly and mightily as their protector and king.

Because of the pitirre, the animals learned that sometimes the smallest of heroes have the biggest hearts. A phrase spread among the creatures: "Cada Guaraguao tiene su Pitirre." A saying that would echo through the island, inspiring resilience in the face of adversity and the hidden strength within us all.

FANTASMA

The campfire crackled and popped as a group of kids huddled close, the glow of the flames attracting all sorts of bugs. It had been a fulfilling day for everyone, and as it came to an end, they wished to go out with a bang. They came prepared with tales, old and new, about phantoms, shades and spooky boos. As the kids' faces danced in the orange light, their eyes sparkled with anticipation of stories that were about to unfold.

Roberto, the youngest, was the first to speak. He leaned in closer to the fire, his voice lowering, hoping to impress the older kids. "Have any of you heard about Jacinto's Well?"

The others looked around, knowing that the story was well known, but they took pity on the newcomer and let him continue, still curious about how he would tell it. He began.

"A long time ago, there was a farmer named Jacinto who lived near Playa Jobos in Isabela. Every day, he'd take his cows to graze like farmers do. Since he was alone and the entire herd would be overwhelming to manage, he took them out to graze one by one. To keep them close, he would tie a rope, one side attached to the cows, the other tied around his waist. For the most part, the system worked. But one rainy day, thunder cracked the sky, and one of his cows got spooked. It ran hard, dragging Jacinto behind it. He struggled to stop the cow as it swept across mud, grass, and stone. As they approached the coast, Jacinto got worried because they were headed to a dead end. Despite the impending doom, the cow didn't stop. It continued until it fell into a deep pit nestled between the ocean rocks. They crashed into the water, and the waves enveloped them. They were lost to the sea forever."

Roberto paused, scanning the other to gauge their interest before continuing. "But if you go to the strange rock formation that we now call a well and shout, 'Jacinto, dame la vaca!' you'll hear the waves crash violently in response. Some say Jacinto's spirit still lingers within the confines of the well and its waves, angry and upset about the way that he died and how everyone has been mocking him ever since. So, if you ever find yourself near Jacinto's well, I wouldn't recommend calling out to him to ask for his cow because he might just wash you away… to eternally join him in the well alongside the ghost of his cow."

The others sat still, impressed by his delivery. Then, a girl across from him broke the silence. Daniela was her name, and she was always a pain.

"That's not even scary," she said, her voice condescending and unserious.

Roberto shot back, "Well, you guys said we were telling ghost stories, not 'scary' stories, so excuse me. If you think you can do better, go ahead. You're next."

Daniela didn't hesitate. She cleared her throat, and with a mischievous smile, she began.

"I know for a fact that you have never heard of the La Francesca de San Rafael."

The kids shook their heads. Apart from San Rafael being a cemetery, they'd never heard of the mysterious woman she mentioned.

"There's a legend about a French noblewoman who came to be buried in a now-unmarked grave of San Rafael. She lived a life of wealth and luxury with her daughter and never knew any suffering or misfortune. That was, of course, until the Great White Plague arrived. No amount of money could have saved you from the simple yet wicked disease that plagued the island. The French women, along with other nobles and diplomats, locked themselves in their apartments above the chaos of the streets and held parties while those below died.

"One evening, they decided to invite an opera singer from abroad to perform for them in their hall. The performance was a revelation, but unbeknownst to everyone there, she was sick and her song carried the disease. Not long after, the French woman's daughter succumbed to tuberculosis and died.

"The French woman had never felt pain like this before, and her body simply couldn't handle the distress. She died of a broken heart. In her death, the French woman was hopeful she'd be reunited with her daughter, but the poor girl was never buried near her mother. This insult drove the French woman's spirit into madness.

"Since then, every night, she rises from her grave and wanders the cemetery, singing lullabies to her lost daughter, still hoping to one day find her. If she can't find her…I guess she'll settle for any other girl who crosses her path to take her daughter's place. No one dares enter that cemetery after sunset, especially young girls… not unless they're looking to get adopted."

Everyone around the circle was reluctant to be impressed, but it was a good story. So much so that it inspired Lucas. He raised his hand eagerly.

"Can I go next?"

The others turned toward him, and he began, his voice a little shaky and nervous.

"This is the story about the Desmembrados." Luca swallowed heavily, then continued. "It's a gruesome phenomenon that often happens in Lajas, on the PR-116. It begins at night, always at night. The event is signaled by the frantic barking of dogs, but none can be seen. The barking is like a herald, a warning about what is about to happen. And then it begins. Arms, legs, torsos, and drag themselves and roll across the length of the road as if they'd been ripped apart and now had a will of their own.

"Everyone knows who these limbs belong to. It's quite obvious when you look closely. The glass fragments, the consistent bruising, it could only mean one thing. They are the dismembered souls of those who died in car accidents on that very stretch of road…still roaming, lost, just trying to get home. I swear I saw it myself, the bodies scattered across the road, going forth as if they were alive. Trying aimlessly to reach their destination. But come morning, they're gone. There is no one except the witnesses to say otherwise."

Daniela interjected, looking a little skeptical. "You definitely haven't seen that happen."

Luca ignored her and addressed another one of his friends. "You should go next, Erick. You're good at this."

Eager to share his own story, Erick quickly jumped in.

"Let me tell you about a fisherman from Orocovis. He was known for fishing all day, and usually all the way into the night. He'd often have to walk back home from his fishing spot through the forest in the darkness. Knowing this, he often brought a stick and a cloth to make a torch to light the way. One night, though, something went wrong. His torch burned out quicker than usual. Afraid of getting lost, he tried to use some of the branches around him, but the wood was too wet to catch fire. He was desperate, so he looked in his bag for something useful. Underneath the fish guts and equipment, he found a wooden crucifix, a holy ornament left to him by his late father. It was the only flammable thing in his possession."

"Despite his better judgment, he lit the crucifix on fire, hoping it was enough to guide him home. It worked. He made it home just as the last of the cross had burnt away, and he believed he was safe. But the next day, he got sick; so sick, he died from his illness. People began to say he died from a curse, a punishment from God for burning a holy symbol.

"Even in death, the fisherman found no rest. It's said that God gave him an impossible task to complete if he was ever going to be allowed into heaven. He was to roam the island until he gathered every last flake of ash of the crucifix he burned. People still report seeing a glowing light flicker among the trees. It's him, the poor fisherman's soul, still searching for the ashes."

The kids were quiet. Luca was right, Erick was good at telling stories.

The last girl to speak, Juliana, said, "I guess it's my turn." Her voice was a whisper. "It's about the Graduation Ghost of Yauco. I don't know if you know it or not, but here we go."

The others leaned in, for it was the last story of the dwindling night.

"A girl went to her graduation party and had the time of her life. At the party, she met a boy and they both danced the night away. He was the perfect gentleman the entire time, and when the night was over, he offered to drive her home. On the way, he noticed she seemed cold, so he gave her his jacket. When they got to her house, she kissed him on the cheek and walked inside, taking the jacket with her. The boy had such a good time that he believed he might have fallen in love. He felt lucky that she had forgotten to return the jacket because it meant he could come pick it up tomorrow, and he would get to see her again. The next day, he returned to her house for his jacket, but when he knocked on the door, an older woman answered. He spoke to her and found out that she was the girl's mother. The boy introduced himself and mentioned that he was looking for her daughter. The girl's mother shook her head.

'My daughter died a few years ago. Are you sure you have the right house, son?'

"This new information made his blood run cold. How was this possible? The girl he danced with, the girl he'd kissed, was already dead. Was the encounter all in his head? Or was there something bigger going on? He described the girl in detail, and her mother showed him pictures of her dead daughter. Seeing the pictures confirmed it was the same girl.

"In order to be absolutely sure, the boy visits the girl's supposed grave. Sure enough, he was greeted with a surprise. Atop her gravestone lay his jacket along with a note that said, 'Thank you for the amazing night.' He put the jacket on, stuffed the note in his pocket, and soberly headed home. Knowing the things he wished he didn't know, the boy hung his head low as he walked."

The kids sat in stunned silence. At this point, the flames of the campfire were almost extinguished, and the sun was creeping on the horizon. Finally, Roberto spoke.

"I didn't realize there were so many ghosts on this island."

With a genuine smile, Daniela responded, "You haven't even scratched the surface. There's plenty more to tell from secret corners across Puerto Rico... but we've run out of the cover of night. It's time to turn down before the sun comes up. We'll save the rest for later."

The others agreed. They curled up in their sleeping bags and drifted off to sleep. The fire dwindled and died, and the sun rose to replace it. As the sun arced higher in the sky and the light caressed the children, they began to fade away with the shadows and the nighttime. It wasn't long before the children and their camping gear completely disappeared.

Later, a guide was leading a group of tourists through the empty campsite. He recounted a tragic historical tale about a group of kids who disappeared there. They had come to sit under the stars to tell each other ghost stories, but were never seen again.

BRUJA

Maitea stood in front of the mirror, a reflection of her former self she no longer knew. The last time she'd cried over love had been two months ago, but it felt like a lifetime. Another relationship, another failure. The truth was simple: she was done with heartache, done with broken promises; most of all, she was done hoping.

The text had come while she was cleaning up a broken plate. *This isn't gonna work out.* He had said it with such ease. Disbelief struck. She was certain that they were in love. She always thought so. When the sobs subsided, she packed her things and left the city behind, returning to the only place she could think of: home. The home she had left for a better life in the States. A life she never found. One might think it irrational and immature to uproot your entire life after a breakup, but sometimes a drastic leap is needed for a significant change in fate.

Her grandmother's house wasn't much. A tiny place on the outskirts of Arecibo, engulfed by shrubbery and wind chimes. Occasionally, there was a chicken sighting. The outdoors smelled like passion fruit and wild garlic, while the inside of the house smelled like incense and rosemary. It was here she hoped to restart her life. Her grandmother, a short woman with beautiful silvery hair styled in a bun, came out to welcome her precious *nieta* home.

"Abu, I'm done," Maitea said, collapsing into an old wicker chair. "I give up on life, on everything. I'll just mooch off of you from now on. Is that okay?"

Her grandmother, who was not a woman known to waste words, laughed. "Don't worry, your Abu is going to fix everything." She cradled her granddaughter's head and brought her inside.

That night, after an evening cup of coffee, the old woman told her about a spell, an ancient one.

"The Witch's Brew," her grandmother told her. "It is a spell that can help any woman, any witch, find true love."

Maitea shook her head, skeptical. "Abu, you still think you're a witch? When I was little, I assumed it was a phase or, you know, a lifestyle choice. I don't believe in that stuff."

"You don't believe? I thought we taught you better than that. With how bad you tell me your life is, it sounds like magic would be the only solution. Trust me. What do you have to lose?"

Abu handed her a tattered old list.

"We require four things: Flor de Maga, *plumas de colibrí*, *hojas* Kalanchoe, and *lágrimas hechiceras*. Find them, bring them to me, and I promise you'll get what you're looking for."

"How am I supposed to get those things? It's not like they sell any of it at the grocery store. Besides, I don't even have a car."

"Problems beget solutions, my dear," she said. "You'll need help, let me think… Oh! Remember Garcia from elementary school? He still lives on the next street over."

"That nerd that I would make fun of on the playground? I don't think so," Maitea said.

"Garcia lived on the island his entire life, unlike you. He is a professor now, which means he has smarts. He has a *car*, and more importantly, would be willing to help. Hey, I'll even get you started. Why don't you head to Guyana for the first ingredient?"

Maitea agreed to ask Garcia for help, despite remembering that Garcia was the one person she couldn't stand when she was younger. A professor? He'd always been too smart for his own good, too quick to correct, and far too sarcastic for her taste. Something that she couldn't quite place annoyed her to the point of acting out. Maybe a feeling of inadequacy in the classroom or perhaps fear of gradeschool cooties. All she knew was that they had clashed enough times as children; she couldn't imagine how much worse it would be now that they were adults.

Despite her reservations, she knew she needed help. She walked to his house and rang the bell. The man who answered the door was not the man she had expected. He looked nothing like the annoying kid she once knew. Garcia had grown into his features with a wise and rugged aura about him. He was, dare she think it, handsome. But she couldn't get distracted. The faster she collected what she needed, the faster she might get what she wanted.

"I need you to take me to Guyana," she said, with a mix of frustration and resignation. He looked back in surprise.

"Excuse me?"

"Please?"

Garcia crosses his arms in front of his chest and stares her down. Maitea feels like a specimen under his microscope, the way he observes her. Like if he was remembering every nasty thing she ever said or did to him. Maitea blushes. Garcia's eyes soften, if just for a moment. It has always been suspected that he had a schoolboy crush on her.

"Fine. But only because I'm a nice guy."

He granted her wish and accepted the challenge. Soon they were both in the car and on their way. Their journey was off to an irksome start. The sun bore down with an intensity that made everything feel slow and sticky. When their car broke down halfway through the journey, they were forced to walk in the sweltering heat that Maitea was unaccustomed to. In order to break the tension, Garcia tried to open up the conversation.

"So, Guyana?" he said, raising an eyebrow. "The land of witches. You know, they say people who take from the land are cursed in kind. Whatever it is you're looking for…"

"Are you kidding me?" Maitea snapped, cutting him off, wiping the sweat from her brow. "Why does everything bad have to happen to me? It's just not natural to be this hot. How are you not dying?"

Garcia smirked. "I'm fine. Maybe the universe is just trying to tell you something."

They argued all the way into the town. Maitea was certain the villagers would hear them coming, but when they finally arrived, the town was empty. Guyana was colorful, filled with lively nature and a mysterious energy, but it was desolate and unkempt.

"What, exactly, are we here for?" asked Garcia, staring out at the empty town.

With a huff, Maitea produced the list of ingredients. Garcia pointed at the word 'Kalanchoe' and revealed that it had another, more commonly used name: witches' hazel, or the witch's leaf. In fact, the town of Guyana was known to be home to a robust population of that wild-growing plant.

The pair walked around the town until Garcia spotted a bushel of the bright red flowers growing in a small garden at the back of the old woman's house. Unafraid of a little old woman or Garcia's warning about curses, Maitea strode through the gate of the garden, pulled a couple of leaves, and ran. Garcia followed her.

As they waited for their car to be towed and fixed, Garcia went on and on about the plant's history and significance with the kind of enthusiasm she had never seen from him before. "It's said that the plant thrives only when tended with love. It's a symbol of persistence and patience."

Maitea nodded. Her thumb stroked one of the leaves, kneading it to softness. She couldn't help but smile.

Through the grace of the skilled mechanic, their car was fixed. Their journey was back underway. Maitea returned to the list and found herself back at square one. Where were they supposed to find the rest of these ingredients, which now seemed even harder to come by in comparison?

"Leave it to me," Garcia said, cranking the car into gear.

He ended up taking her to the Luquillo Wildlife Research Center, which was the perfect place to search for the elusive and impossible hummingbird feather.

Maitea was eager to find the feather as quickly as possible, so she dropped to her knees and scanned the floor, keeping an eye out for the bright spark of a hummingbird feather. After what seemed like hours of looking, Maitea finally broke the silence.

"Have you found anything?" she asked.

When Garcia didn't answer, she stood and looked around the enclosure. To her surprise, Garcia was a few feet away from her. He stood still, arms outstretched like a scarecrow, with a kaleidoscope of winged friends perched comfortably on his body.

"Help!" he whimpered to Maitea with a smile. She couldn't help but laugh, which caused the birds to scatter, with the whir of their tiny wings sending feathers flying all around them.

"You're like a bird magnet," she said.

Garcia looked over at her, a genuine smile forming on his face. He finally lowered his arms.

"Guess I have a way with creatures." Suddenly, his smile was replaced with a frown. "You have something in your hair."

He moved in to pick a hummingbird feather from her hair.

"One more down, two to go," she said.

Garcia handed her the feather, and when their hands touched, Maitea felt something stir inside her. It was as if a firework had gone off in her chest. For the first time, Maitea looked at Garcia and saw him as more than just the smart-ass teacher or classmate. She saw him as… someone else. Someone interesting. And despite herself, she found the whole situation strangely comforting.

Garcia spoke of the famous tale of Alida and Taroo, a pair of Taino lovers; one cursed to be a flower and the other a hummingbird, fated to try every flower until he found his other half.

"Does Taroo ever find Alida?" asked Maitea.

"We don't know," said Garcia. "But I'd like to think so. If their love was strong enough, I bet Taroo tasted every single flower on the island till he found Alida. I know if I loved someone like that, that's what I would do."

With the witch's hazel and hummingbird feather procured, they were off to find their next ingredient. To find La Flor de Maga, they decided to travel to the University of Puerto Rico's Botanical Gardens.

Maitea and Garcia did their best to blend into the crowd. As they walked among the gardens in search of the plant, Garcia shared the tragic tale of the witch who died in its creation. Maitea listened intently, drawn into his words.

"La Flor de Maga is derived from a young witch. She hid in a tree to get away from the conquistadors, but they buried an arrow in her throat and killed her. From her spilled blood sprang the first Flor de Maga blooms."

Garcia lightly touches Maitea's arm and points to a bright red flower. Maitea has never seen so rich a red on a flower before. Her fingers itch to touch it.

"The flower is a symbol of sacrifice and feminine powers," Garcia said, gazing at the red petals.

For a moment, Maitea forgot about their differences and incompatibilities. She forgot the ultimate goal of this entire pilgrimage. In that moment, she realized that she wasn't just gathering ingredients to find love and happiness. She was gathering pieces of herself along the way that she once thought lost.

They picked the flower and put it with the rest of their items. Now they only had one last ingredient to procure, *las lágrimas hechiceras,* the most elusive of them all.

Maitea looked to Garcia, her heart hopeful that they would fulfill the last stretch of their journey.

"Where to next?" she asked.

But this time, Garcia didn't have an answer.

"I don't know," he said. "Do you know any witches?"

Maitea shook her head. No, no, no. They were so close to gathering the items that would grant her happiness. Defeated, Maitea sat on a bench. Garcia sat down next to her. Rain clouds began to gather overhead. When the rain finally broke, Maitea felt a sob building in her chest.

"It was a hopeless journey," Maitea muttered. "I will never find happiness."

Such bitter words brought forth Maitea's tears. She retreated into herself, ignoring the rain pelting her head and pooling in her cradled hands. She barely moved when Garcia put his arm around her shaking shoulders.

"Do you know where the rain comes from?" asked Garcia.

Maitea shook her head. She didn't care about the rain; she could only focus on her failure.

"Here in Puerto Rico, we say that when it rains like this, it is a witch's wedding day. Witches are often left at the altar, and so, they are weeping for the groom who never came. The rain, this rain... I think it's what your *abuela* meant when she wrote down the witch's tears."

Maitea swallowed her tears and looked up. The rain fell on her face, light as kisses. She laughed, a sound full of relief. Together, they grabbed an empty water bottle to catch the water. It didn't matter that their clothes were soaked through, and it didn't matter that Garcia used to be the nerdy boy she couldn't tolerate. Without thinking, she got up on her tippy toes and they shared a soft, sweet, and passionate kiss.

When they pulled apart, they were both breathless, their faces flushed with unexpected surprise.

"I...I'm sorry, don't know why I did that," Maitea said, embarrassed, her heart still pounding in her chest.

"Must be the witch's tears," Garcia responded.

Freaked out, Maitea quickly shut the situation down. "Let's just forget about it, okay?"

Maitea got into the car before he could answer. They drove back in silence. Maitea sprang out of the car without so much as a goodbye. The second her feet were safely on the ground, Garcia sped off.

Maitea walked slowly and confused to the front door. Once inside, she handed over the ingredients to her grandmother and watched as the old woman slowly organized everything for the witch's brew. Before the first ingredient could be added, Maitea grabbed her grandmother's wrist.

"Wait! I'm not sure I want this anymore," she exclaimed.

Her grandmother raised an eyebrow. "Why not?"

"I... I don't know... It's not... I think I like Garcia." Her voice faltered, but she stood firm.

Her grandmother's face softened, and she placed a hand on Maitea's shoulder. "Thank God. I have no idea what I would have done if you had to drink this bullshit."

"Why, why would you make me do all these pointless things?"

Her grandmother smiled. "Pointless? Only you and you alone could break the curse you put over yourself." Maitea stood frozen for a moment, the weight of the revelation settling over her. Then, she blurted out, "What curse? You just said that all this was a lie and that you made me do all this for nothing. Are you insane?"

Her grandmother responded, disappointed with Maitea's lack of self-awareness. "Wise women with power are often called insane, but let me ask you something... it worked, didn't it? Didn't your path lead you to beautiful places all over the island, reacquainting you with the island that you left so long ago? Did your travel companion not teach you the stories and histories that are imprinted in your blood? Did you not find love?

"Magic is real... You just never needed it. If it weren't, how would I know that your future lies beyond that door?" She pointed to the front door of the house.

Maitea wiped off the tears that were beginning to bubble up and headed to the door. She was skeptical now after all that had happened, but curious and hopeful. She opened the door, and there he was. She found Garcia outside, standing as if ready to ring the bell.

Unprepared, he began to mutter, "Hi, Maitea. I just wanted to...?" Maitea cut him off. This time, she didn't hesitate. She kissed him again, clear-headed and without regrets.

"Guess I underestimated Abu for the last time. Uh, what happens now?" Maitea said, excited for the endless futures she could now see in front of her.

Garcia grinned. "I think we both learned a lot in the past couple of days. How about we just see where the 'magic' takes us?" And for the first time in a long while, Maitea felt her life fall into place and that she was exactly where she was meant to be.

They held each other together for quite a while, her grandmother providing no privacy. When they pulled apart, there was no awkwardness, only the understanding that sometimes, the most powerful magic is simply being in the moment. And that love, the right kind of love, will make itself known if you let it in.

"Monstruo"- Digital Art From the Coay collection (2024) -

MONSTRUO

As a child, I was afraid of the dark. There was always a collection of shapes and sounds coming in and out of the unknown, summoning all sorts of evil to haunt me. I didn't always see them, not at first. But as I grew older, they were always there, lurking in the darkness just outside my window. I'd lie awake in bed and stare at shifting, dark, and amorphous silhouettes, waiting for something to jump out at me. Something was out there. I knew it. I felt it. And sometimes, I'd even catch a glimpse of those glowing red eyes stalking me.

When I told my parents, they laughed.

"It's the Cuco, *hijo,*" they'd say, skeptical and dismissive. "If you don't stop your whining and go to bed, *el Cuco te va a comer,*" they'd say. As if mocking me would make me feel better. It never did. They thought it was all in my head, that I was just scared of shadows and other irrational childhood fears. But they didn't understand. I wasn't afraid of the shadows themselves, but what lurked and hid within them.

I wouldn't stop talking about it. I'd cry, insist, and beg, anything to make my parents see what I did. They didn't believe me, of course. When my behavior continued, when I refused to stop obsessing over these monsters that plagued my nights, my parents took me to a

109

therapist. I was a teenager by then, and my obsession with the shadows had only grown stronger. But I knew that if I made my feelings known, everyone would think I was crazy. The therapist chalked it up to "childhood delusions," and my parents decided I was just "too imaginative for my own good."

As I grew older, I learned to keep quiet. People didn't want to hear about what I thought was true. So, I buried it. I lived with it quietly, constantly looking over my shoulder and surveying the unknown and undesirable for signs of otherworldly life. No matter what everyone said or what society believed, I couldn't let it go. It still haunted me. I went to college and decided to write my thesis on the unknown and the creatures that lurk just beyond our understanding. I spent months researching and compiling evidence of testimonials and eyewitness accounts. I knew there was something out there. The world was full of mysteries, and I was determined to uncover them.

I titled my thesis, *The Monsters of Puerto Rican Lore.* I thought if I could show the world the evidence, if I could prove I wasn't crazy, people would finally understand. I buried my knowledge, my experiences, everything I had into this one truly remarkable exposé, confident that it was detailed, comprehensive, convincing, and incontestable.

But when I presented my thesis, the professors doubled over laughing. They mocked me for believing in such nonsense. "You've got to be kidding," they said. The assessment was a failure, and I realized that, once again, I had been proven wrong in their eyes. I knew I'd reached my breaking point.

I was done hiding. I was old enough now to make my own way and think for myself. I wasn't crazy, and I was going to prove it. All I needed was incontrovertible, undeniable evidence. And I knew I would have to find it myself.

I grabbed all the money I had saved up, packed my bags, and set out, determined and focused. My old research had pointed me to several places in Puerto Rico—places steeped in legend and fear. First, I went to Barceloneta to find the elusive Gargola. There were several recent eyewitness accounts, so the chances of my finding something were high. Many locals had reported seeing a gargoyle-like creature snatch people up off the streets in the middle of the night. Witnesses said it was a big gray creature that smelled of sulfur, with massive talons and wings. It would perch atop buildings and stalk people below, waiting for the moment to snatch one away, coming and going, leaving no trace other than the disappeared victim. With binoculars, I attentively watched for days from my motel room window, waiting for any movement or news. I also set up a recording camera at the window across the room, hoping it would see something if I missed it. It didn't. The nights passed by slowly, and staying awake took practice, but I forced myself to do it. But after several days of stakeouts, there was nothing. No sign of the creature anywhere. I tried talking to the witnesses, but they were not eager to talk to me, a crazy stranger. I couldn't waste any more time and resources, so I moved on to the next subject.

I then traveled to the hills of Moca to find the infamous giant white vampire bat. *El Vampiro de Moca*, they'd call it, a creature that often came in the night to feed on any living thing it could find, draining them of blood and leaving the empty carcasses for everyone to see. The witness statements were aligned and conclusive. It was said to be a very large vampire bat, the color of spoiled milk. I first hung nets in the trees, hoping to trap it mid-flight. They were attached to a rope with cans on the ends that were meant to rattle and alert me of any disturbance. I then prepared a small camp for myself, making sure to put out all the lights so as to not scare it away. I camped out in the forest, using myself as bait. I'd lie awake looking up at the stars, jumping at any noise I heard beyond my periphery. But after a week of waiting and surviving on the little supplies I had, I realized it was another dead end. There were no signs of the creature. Nothing but the silence of the forest. No vampire. No proof.

Then, as a last resort, I went to a part of the island where there was nothing but open plains and fincas, where there were many reports of the *Chupacabra*. Although many countries came to adopt the belief in the gruesome creature, its origin was Puerto Rico. After cross-referencing my research, I found the perfect location to lure it out. It was said to be a bloodthirsty creature that had been attacking livestock for years, even centuries. It was described as smooth, ranging in pale to dark tones, with a big jaw full of sharp teeth and spikes all along its back. I doubted I could hunt this beast down with my bare hands, so I obsessed over setting a trap and recording it all. With the last of my money, I bought a goat and set it up as bait. I placed it under a large cage

112

that I had rigged to fall when appropriate, trapping the creature. I positioned everything accordingly and watched from a secure area under a fake bush. Once again, I waited, exhausting my memory card and my sanity. I found nothing. No creature. No evidence. All this time and effort wasted.

I had risked everything, my money, security, social life, and future, for what? I began to question if what I had believed my entire life was just a product of my own mind. Maybe the monsters weren't real. Maybe it was all in my head. Penniless and with nowhere else to turn, I went back home to my parents' house, where this all began. I knew that no matter how strange our relationship had become, they loved me and would greet me with open arms.

I arrived at their house and confessed what had happened, apologizing for not taking their advice sooner. I asked for their forgiveness, and with a mixture of love and pity, they gave it. We shared a sad but satisfying hug, then they helped me get my bags inside.

That night, as I lay in my childhood bed, I couldn't sleep. My mind was racing with a stew of fear, disappointment, failure, and regret. That is when it happened. The room began to grow colder. The windows rattled, and there was a low humming sound in the air. I looked around, confused, and then I saw it. At the foot of my bed, a shadowy figure began to rise. Those glowing red eyes stared right at me. The figure grew taller and shifted forms until it resembled something close to human.

It bent over my bed until it was directly over me and said, "Hello."

Its voice echoed in the room, low and unnerving, filling it with a sinister undertone. I couldn't believe it. My parents had accidentally stumbled upon the truth all those years ago. It was *El Cuco.*

I was paralyzed by fear. My body wouldn't move, even though my head and my heart wanted to run away. I wanted to scream, to get out of that room, but I couldn't. Before I could fully process, the nightmarish creature began to speak again.

"You've been a very bad boy," it said. "You've snitched, you've meddled, and you tried to lure us out in the open. You almost got us found out." Its eyes glowed brighter. "For that, poor boy, you must be punished."

As I whimpered, the Cuco seemed to stretch, its shape contorting. "Don't worry, hurting you wouldn't be any fun, but I brought some friends with me; ones I believe you are already familiar with," it hissed. "Maybe you should check on mommy and daddy. They might believe you now."

And then, just like that, the figure was gone.

I leapt out of bed, my heart skipping every other beat, and ran down the hall to my parents' room. The door creaked open. What I saw made my throat recoil and my stomach convulse.

There, situated snugly on their bed, were the creatures I had spent my best years hunting: La Gargola, el Vampiro de Moca, and el Chupacabra; they were real. I had no time to celebrate that I had been right all along because there they stood, over my parents' bodies, their teeth coated in fresh blood.

I screamed. The creatures turned, startled. My panic sent them into a frenzy. One of them slashed my forearm with their fishhook claws. They ran, smashing through the window and fleeing into the night, leaving me with a ripped sleeve and a deep, pulsing gash in my skin. I chased after them, but I was too slow. How could human legs compete with their wild and beastly ways?

I called the police, panicked and breathless. When they arrived, the house was eerily silent. To my surprise, once at the scene of the attack, my parents' bed was clean, and the window intact. There was no blood. No bodies. Nothing once again. What had happened? I was defeated, awake, and the pain I felt was real, so why must I suffer under others' skepticism? Why must I be forced to question myself?

After talking to the neighbors, the officer, in an upset tone, informed me that my parents had been on a cruise, celebrating their retirement for the better part of a week. They'd not been home the entire time, which brought up countless more questions and concerns. After a thorough investigation and a stern talking-to, the officer let me off with a warning, recommending that I seek professional help, and if I were to call again, I'd be arrested immediately.

There it was. I had heard too many doubts, so maybe they were right. It was all just in my head. Maybe I'm the one who's…

I suddenly looked down at my intact sleeve and pulled it up, revealing the gash on my arm that was still there and throbbing; a wound clearly not left by anything human, but like a signature clawed into me by something truly monstrous. Confused and disillusioned, I went back inside and prayed that the memory of the events of that night and the many before would fade away, leaving me in peaceful bliss.

Many years later, trying and failing to forget and completely move on, I led a pretty boring life. Since that night, everything had seemed grayish and stagnant in the air. The difference between light and dark, reality and fantasy, was a blur. The only thing I could see clearly was the many faces of evil. I know what I saw. I know what I felt, for the scar on my arm reminded me of it every day.

If there's one thing I've learned, it's that there is much we don't know about this world, mysteries and fictions seeded in reality, waiting to reveal themselves. I've come to understand that nightmares are real, even though we try to deny and hide from them. We can either live in fear or fight them head-on.

NIEVE

Once upon a time, in the capital of Puerto Rico, there lived a young girl named Marisol. She grew up in the warmth of the sun and the fragrance of tropical flowers, fried foods, and spices. Despite this, there was one thing Marisol longed for more than anything else in the world: snow. She often felt jealous of those who had the opportunity to witness the consequences of winter, blind to how fortunate she was.

Marisol had seen it many times on her parents' television, glittering and white, falling gently from the sky. Those typical American movies made it seem so tantalizing and fun. It was a sight so far removed from the island life she knew, where the sun never stopped shining and winters got no colder than 70 degrees. The snowball fights, s'mores, and smiles seemed like an unattainable fantasy. Impossible as it might have seemed, she still used up all her prayers, birthday wishes, and shooting stars to ask for the same thing.

Every year, as Christmas approached, she would sit by the window and watch the distant stars twinkle, wondering what a white Christmas would look like. This Christmas was no different, and so she knelt down by her bed and prayed to God, asking for just one chance to see snow in her lifetime. It wasn't important how long or how much; she only wanted a moment to live her dream. She went to bed that night unsure if God had heard her.

The next morning, she sat on her porch with her mother as they had breakfast, when out of nowhere she heard a strange noise. Marisol noticed the unfamiliar hum getting louder and louder coming from the bright blue sky. She looked up and saw something flying overhead. It could've been a plane, but it was so small, Marisol couldn't be sure. It passed quite quickly, but something had clearly happened because the sky seemed to blur.

Suddenly, tiny white shavings began to fall from the sky, drifting down onto everything and everyone. Snow! It was snow, real snow, falling over the capital city. Marisol gasped in wonder. God had been listening after all.

She ran into the road, children and adults alike following suit. They spun in joy as they danced beneath the flurries, catching whatever snowflakes they could on their tongues. The snowflakes that fell to the ground dotted the pavement from one, wonderful moment before melting in the tropical heat.

Marisol didn't care. She built snowmen she could in the time she had, saddened as she watched them slowly fade away. The fun might have been momentary, but the joy would last a lifetime. It was perfect. For a moment, her dream had come true.

When Marisol headed back inside her home and exclaimed to her mother, "Mami, did you feel it? Wasn't it amazing?"

Her mother smiled warmly and nodded.

"Yes, *mi amor*, it was beautiful. Makes me wonder what else the new mayor has up her sleeve. I always knew that Felisa Rincón was something special."

Confused, Marisol was quick to correct her mother, "What do you mean, *mami*? I was the one who was responsible for the snow. I prayed and prayed, and now it finally came."

"No, no *cariño*. Planes dropped the snow. It was all arranged by our new mayor. She meant to impress us, and I think she has."

But Marisol shook her head, full of resolve and faith. "No, Mami, that is just not true. It was a gift from God. I know it was."

Her mother sighed softly, a look of love and pity across her face. "I know you believe that Marisol and I'm glad you have such a strong relationship with the lord. But there is a difference between facts and miracles."

Marisol was steadfast and would not be swayed. She held onto the belief and knowledge. It was a miracle, a sign that God had heard her. She grew up with the certainty that, one day, snow would fall on Puerto Rico again.

Years passed, and Marisol grew into a young woman, then an adult. But the snow never returned to the island. She never stopped believing that God had a hand in the miracle, but she began to believe that maybe her mom also had a point. Who's to say how God's power manifests on earth? Maybe he inspired the mayor to make it snow, knowing it would answer her prayers. Maybe it was all part of a more intricate tapestry of events, and people were compelled to walk the path that was laid out. Whatever the case, she thought, *Who am I to try to make sense of these impossible things? I was just a girl whose dream came true. And I'm happy with that.*

Marisol lived her life with a quiet hope within her. She traveled the world, lived through many Christmases, and experienced the cold winters of faraway lands. Yet, in her heart, she always held on to that one perfect moment, the miracle of snow in Puerto Rico.

BOMBA

Rey lived in Vieques, a charming little town by the beach. Despite his youth, he was a quiet, mature, and focused ten-year-old with an old soul. When he wasn't playing with his friends, he loved to play bomba on his *barril*, a hand drum used in Afro-Puerto Rican music. He often joined a group of retirees in the square, where they spent their days playing dominoes, smoking cigars, and making music. Bomba was more than just a rhythm on a drum; it was a conversation between the dancer and the drummer. It reminded Rey of the natural world around him: the swaying trees, the beating waves. Each movement in nature seemed to respond to an unseen rhythm, just like in his music.

On Saturdays, Rey would practice his bomba in solitude. Instead of using dancers, he would follow the rhythms of nature with his *sicá* and *holandés*. But one Saturday, his peace was interrupted by his friends, eager to drag him to the beach to play soccer and build sandcastles. Rey smiled, thinking to himself, *What a life we have here.*

The sun was shining brightly, and the beach was the center of their paradise. As they were having fun, Rey noticed a group of classmates gathered near a hole in the sand, their faces filled with curiosity. When he went over to investigate, he found Talia, one of his classmates, holding a strange black object. It looked old and mysterious, its purpose unclear. But everyone could tell it was something designed with care. Talia, knowing Rey to be the most responsible of them all, handed it to him. At that moment, Rey's mom appeared, calling him for lunch. Her eyes widened in horror when she saw the object in his hands.

"Put that down! Now!" she shouted, rushing toward the children. Rey dropped the object back into the hole. His mother's face was stern as she ordered all the children to go home, forbidding them from returning to the beach.

Once home, Rey asked his mom why she was so upset. She sighed and told him that he may have a gift for music, but his head was often in the clouds.

"The island has always been a strategic port, perfectly situated between the old world and the new. During the Spanish colonial era, Puerto Rico was used as a military hub. Even after the Spanish were driven out and the U.S. took control, the weapons left behind were the consequences of war. The object you found was a leftover landmine from those days. Even though they are said to be inactive, it's dangerous to mess with things like that. They didn't care to clean up after themselves, and now, it's left for us to deal with."

Rey asked why nothing had been done to fix it.

"The island's people are too busy, too poor. There aren't enough resources to clean up what was left behind," his mom said.

But Rey wasn't convinced. He couldn't shake the thought of the beach, his beloved home, being a place of danger, a place to be feared. How could he play music or feel free when something as menacing as a landmine might be buried under his feet?

Determined to do something about it, Rey gathered his friends and classmates, explaining what his mother had told him. Together, they made a plan to clean up the beach. They were determined to play in the sand like their ancestors once did, joyful and carefree.

But how would they find the landmines? That's when Talia interjected with an idea. Every town has a crazy old uncle, and in their town, it was Don Ignacio. Rey and his friends had seen him rummaging through trash, scavenging, and hustling his way through life. He didn't particularly like children, but it was a risk they were willing to take. If anyone knew how to solve their problem, it was him.

They went to Don Ignacio's house. He answered the door with an annoyed grunt, but when they explained their mission, he listened.

"You'll need a metal detector," he told them. "But you kids won't be able to afford one, let alone clear away the debris from years of neglect."

Rey, ever clever, suggested they could make one themselves. "I'll bet a smart and savvy man like you knows how to build a makeshift metal detector," Rey said, his eyes sparkling with irritating wonder.

Don Ignacio waved a dismissive hand, but Rey kept pressing him. He even offered to steal a few beers from his mother's fridge as payment. Don Ignacio finally agreed. He didn't want to contribute to any potential chaos they might get up to, but he couldn't say no to defending his pride.

Don Ignacio guided them through the basics of metal detectors, helping them gather materials: coils, capacitors, resistors, and oscillators. With his help, they built five rickety detectors, far from perfect and barely functional, but good enough. Armed with their makeshift tools, the children returned to the beach, shovels in hand and wagons ready for whatever they might dig up.

They worked in groups, sweeping the sand back and forth. Whenever the detectors beeped, they dug furiously, collecting what seemed like an endless array of war debris: old explosives, artillery shells, and beach mines. Nearby tourists stopped their sunbathing and began filming and taking pictures of the children, as if it were some kind of spectacle. The kids weren't deterred, though. They continued their mission until they had gathered around 19 dangerous objects.

The question of what to do with the objects was put forth.

Rey had an idea. *What if we make the adults finally take responsibility and pay attention?* He thought. They needed to see what their children were doing, how they had taken matters into their own hands, if anything was going to change.

That afternoon, the kids marched to the *plaza pública,* the heart of the town. They dumped their collection of war remnants in the center, making sure the whole town could see what they had unearthed. It wasn't until the next morning that the adults took notice, and all hell broke loose. Frantic, they questioned who had dared to do such a thing. Scared but unashamed, Rey confessed to the deed. The town leaders were in disbelief, and his mother was disappointed and angry. There would be a motherly reckoning for all the children involved.

Elsewhere, the voyeuristic videos of the children's daring feat, filmed by the tourists, were posted online. The videos quickly went viral, spreading beyond the island and capturing the attention of people from around the world. Soon, volunteer groups, NGOs, and bomb experts arrived to clean up the coast at an astonishing pace. The town's people watched from their windows with a mixture of gratitude and resentment.

As the volunteer groups descended, Rey's mother's mood grew darker. She saw the tourists taking pictures of their found objects with captions boasting goodwill and charitableness. What didn't make it into the frame was the overcrowded town that didn't have the capacity for that kind of tourism. Rey's mother couldn't stand how cramped and noisy the town had become. What she wished most of all was to hear some of her son's beautiful music, but his *barril* had gone silent. Rey had been in his room since the day of the incident, and it was like he had lost his light.

Eventually, he came out of his room for something to eat. One look at Rey's face told her that he was truly and completely miserable. She took Rey by the hand and marched down to the plaza, where she found a nosy crowd of townspeople looking out toward the beach. She stepped onto a bench, grabbed everyone's attention, and proudly declared the truth she had come to know in her heart.

"We owe my boy an apology. Like many of you, I was blind. But my child–our children–see the possibilities in the world. We are too quick to make excuses. How can we call ourselves Boricuas if we allow this to happen? Aren't you all ashamed that it took outsiders, opportunists, to do the work we should have done long ago? We have been quiet and complacent for far too long. It's time to be the change. This is our beach, our history, and our legacy. Let's do something about it, shall we? Rey! Get your mother a shovel!"

Her words sparked the passions and pride of the townspeople. They rolled up their sleeves, grabbed their tools, and together, they joined the others on the beach. Hope, long buried, was finally rising to the surface. Rey looked upon it all, content, when Thalia tapped him on the shoulder and handed him his *barril.* It was time for some inspirational mood music. He joined the retirees under a palm tree, along with chairs, *pillones,* and a *guiro.* As they played, the sound of bomba filled the air, a triumphant, joyful rhythm, symbolizing the end of a story and the beginning of a new one.

It took months to fully clear the beach, but grain by grain, they did it. It was now safe to play and enjoy once more. After the novelty of it all died down and those who had come to help had gone, the locals were free to return to the warm sand and temperate waters that made up their backyard, a place that felt familiar to them yet changed somehow. The children and adults alike swam, played, ate, and danced; all to the beat of one boy's drum.

Grito Boricua

When I was a boy, in the peak of the 21st century,
Puerto Rico was a different place than it is now. Back
then, the island was struggling, trapped in a dance with a
foreign power that didn't seem to understand us, or want
to. Our economy was broken. We were a people caught
between promises of prosperity that never came. We were
a people shackled by decisions made far from our shores
by people who never set foot on our land. We were a
colony and a state; we were told that we were
'independent,' that we were no one's playthings. But we
were not free.

With unease comes unrest. I remember the
carousel of debate topics: opposing viewpoints on
independence; big business stealing opportunities from
our people; foreigners receiving priority over native born.

I was just a kid, but I always felt deep inside that
we deserved to be more than a jewel in someone else's
empire. More than a favorite vacation destination or a
place to escape one's taxes.

Our anger and frustration manifested into cries of
outrage. When our government didn't hear us, we grew
complacent. Young people, however, have trouble
standing still, and they decide instead to shout louder than

their parents before them. This is when the real change began. The island began to cut its ties. We kicked out the opportunist expats and shut down their golf courses. We shunned the big businesses, and their profit margins began to suffer. Slowly, so slowly, we began to see FOR SALE signs appear on the buildings and businesses that once belonged to the corporate leeches. We took our island back.

Some feared what would come of it. Would we lose favor with the rest of the world for this outlandish attempt at betterment? Could we support our economy? But in those first weeks, as the flags of Puerto Rico flew high and proud, it was clear we knew our future was ours and we were going to break everything in order to rebuild from within.

There were small changes at first. We listened to each other more, especially the elders. Their wise words guided us forth. Our new government began to lift up its youth, especially those with creative and intellectual promise. Those youths grew up to become adults interested in sociology, ecology, and technology. This is when the boom happened.

Our marine biologists returned the color to our coral reefs and bioluminescence to all our waters, sustainably lighting up the night. Scientists brought back the cacophony of sound to our rainforests. We even had some success in bringing some native species back from the brink of extinction. In the countryside, carbon-neutral grazing and expert farming were implemented, thus eliminating food insecurity and dependence on foreign imports. We learned to respect the earth that sustains us and how to give back to it actively.

We mastered how to turn solar power into energy and how to use the wind and water to power our cities. Our cars switched from being gas to electric. The buildings became architectural marvels, perfect for vertical gardens that provided vegetables and fruit, and grew plants that cleaned our air. In the balance that we created, one can feel the heartbeat of the land in our forests, seas, and cities.

We had become so self-sufficient that we developed our own form of currency, *La Estrella*. A fully digital engine of commerce that other countries tried to replicate. Universal healthcare and education paved the way for a safer, healthier, and happier home for all.

In this new age, our people have enough freedom to create. Musical trends in Puerto Rico remain deeply rooted in tradition; salsa, bomba, plena, reggaetón, and even Latin trap stay at the forefront. But these sounds are now blended with new instruments, rhythms, and distinctive Latin techno beats, reflecting our evolution and growth. Across the island, murals cover nearly every wall; vibrant, bold, and full of life. They tell stories of past struggles, of times when we were held down. But they also speak of triumph; of how we rose, reclaimed our power, and built something better for ourselves, for our children, and for the generations to come. Our musicians, artists, and dancers have become the soul of this place. Creativity flows through the island like its rivers, inspiring everyone it touches. The culture, the language, and the very essence of who we are have grown richer, more colorful, and more alive than ever.

We have not just overcome obstacles or survived, but we have flourished. We took what was once broken and turned it into something beautiful, something the world now looks to for inspiration. I think about the struggles, the uncertainty, and how far we've come. Puerto Rico is not just a place on a map anymore. It is a beacon of prosperity and a testament to what Boriquas are capable of. Who, united by love for their land and each other, decided to take control of their own future. And as I watch the younger generation run along the beach wearing clothes made of algae and feathers in their braids, I know one thing for sure: this is just the beginning. The dream has only just begun.

 DI501print

 http://DI501Print.com

 DI501Industries@gmail.com